On the Makaloa Mat: Island Tales

Jack London

CONTENTS:
On the Makaloa Mat
  The Bones of Kahekili
  When Alice Told her Soul
  Shin-Bones
  The Water Baby
  The Tears of Ah Kim
  The Kanaka Surf

John Griffith "Jack" London (born John Griffith Chaney,January 12, 1876 – November 22, 1916)was an American novelist, journalist, and social activist.
John Griffith "Jack" London (born John Griffith Chaney,January 12, 1876 – November 22, 1916)was an American novelist, journalist, and social activist. A pioneer in the then-burgeoning world of commercial magazine fiction, he was one of the first fiction writers to obtain worldwide celebrity and a large fortune from his fiction alone, including science fiction.

Some of his most famous works include The Call of the Wild and White Fang, both set in the Klondike Gold Rush, as well as the short stories "To Build a Fire", "An Odyssey of the North", and "Love of Life". He also wrote of the South Pacific in such stories as "The Pearls of Parlay" and "The Heathen", and of the San Francisco Bay area in The Sea Wolf.

London was part of the radical literary group "The Crowd" in San Francisco and a passionate advocate of unionization, socialism, and the rights of workers. He wrote several powerful works dealing with these topics, such as his dystopian novel The Iron Heel, his non-fiction exposé The People of the Abyss, and The War of the Classes.

On the Makaloa Mat

Unlike the women of most warm races, those of Hawaii age well and nobly. With no pretence of make-up or cunning concealment of time's inroads, the woman who sat under the hau tree might have been permitted as much as fifty years by a judge competent anywhere over the world save in Hawaii. Yet her children and her grandchildren, and Roscoe Scandwell who had been her husband for forty years, knew that she was sixty-four and would be sixty-five come the next twenty-second day of June. But she did not look it, despite the fact that she thrust reading glasses on her nose as she read her magazine and took them off when her gaze desired to wander in the direction of the half-dozen children playing on the lawn.

It was a noble situation--noble as the ancient hau tree, the size of a house, where she sat as if in a house, so spaciously and comfortably house-like was its shade furnished; noble as the lawn that stretched away landward its plush of green at an appraisement of two hundred dollars a front foot to a bungalow equally dignified, noble, and costly. Seaward, glimpsed through a fringe of hundred-foot coconut palms, was the ocean; beyond the reef a dark blue that grew indigo blue to the horizon, within the reef all the silken gamut of jade and emerald and tourmaline.

And this was but one house of the half-dozen houses belonging to Martha Scandwell. Her town-house, a few miles away in Honolulu, on Nuuanu Drive between the first and second "showers," was a palace. Hosts of guests had known the comfort and joy of her mountain house on Tantalus, and of her volcano house, her mauka house, and her makai house on the big island of Hawaii. Yet this Waikiki house stressed no less than the rest in beauty, in dignity, and in expensiveness of upkeep. Two Japanese yard-boys were trimming hibiscus, a third was engaged expertly with the long hedge of night-blooming cereus that was shortly expectant of unfolding in its mysterious night-bloom. In immaculate ducks, a house Japanese brought out the tea-things, followed by a Japanese maid, pretty as a butterfly in the distinctive garb of her race, and fluttery as a butterfly to attend on her mistress. Another Japanese maid, an array of Turkish towels on her arm, crossed the lawn well to the right in the direction of the bath-houses, from which the children, in swimming suits, were beginning to emerge. Beyond, under the palms at the edge of the sea, two Chinese nursemaids, in their pretty native costume of white yee-shon and-straight-lined trousers, their black braids of hair down their backs, attended each on a baby in a perambulator.

And all these, servants, and nurses, and grandchildren, were Martha Scandwell's. So likewise was the colour of the skin of the grandchildren--the unmistakable Hawaiian colour, tinted beyond shadow of mistake by exposure to the Hawaiian sun. One-eighth and one-sixteenth Hawaiian were they, which meant that seven-eighths or fifteen-sixteenths white blood informed that skin yet failed to obliterate the modicum of golden tawny brown of Polynesia. But in this, again, only a trained observer would have known that the frolicking children were aught but pure-blooded white. Roscoe Scandwell, grandfather, was pure white; Martha three-quarters white; the many sons and daughters of them seven-eighths white; the grandchildren graded up to fifteen-sixteenths white, or, in the cases when their seven-eighths fathers and mothers had married seven-eighths, themselves fourteen-sixteenths or seven-eighths white. On both sides the stock was good, Roscoe straight descended from the New England Puritans, Martha no less straight descended from the royal chief-stocks of Hawaii whose genealogies were chanted in males a thousand years before written speech was acquired.

In the distance a machine stopped and deposited a woman whose utmost years might have been guessed as sixty, who walked across the lawn as lightly as a well-cared-for woman of forty, and whose actual calendar age was sixty-eight. Martha rose from her seat to greet her, in the hearty Hawaiian way, arms about, lips on lips, faces eloquent and bodies no less eloquent with sincereness and frank excessiveness of emotion. And it was "Sister Bella," and "Sister Martha," back and forth, intermingled with almost incoherent inquiries about each other, and about Uncle This and Brother That and Aunt Some One Else, until, the first tremulousness of meeting over, eyes moist with tenderness of love, they sat gazing at each other across their teacups. Apparently, they had not seen nor embraced for years. In truth, two months marked the interval of their separation. And one was sixty-four, the other sixty-eight. But the thorough comprehension resided in the fact that in each of them one-fourth of them was the sun-warm, love-warm heart of Hawaii.

The children flooded about Aunt Bella like a rising tide and were capaciously hugged and kissed ere they departed with their nurses to the swimming beach.

"I thought I'd run out to the beach for several days--the trades had stopped blowing," Martha explained.

"You've been here two weeks already," Bella smiled fondly at her younger sister. "Brother Edward told me. He met me at the steamer and insisted on running me out first of all to see Louise and Dorothy and that first grandchild of his. He's as mad as a silly hatter about it."

"Mercy!" Martha exclaimed. "Two weeks! I had not thought it that long."

"Where's Annie?--and Margaret?" Bella asked.

Martha shrugged her voluminous shoulders with voluminous and forgiving affection for her wayward, matronly daughters who left their children in her care for the afternoon.

"Margaret's at a meeting of the Out-door Circle--they're planning the planting of trees and hibiscus all along both sides of Kalakaua Avenue," she said. "And Annie's wearing out eighty dollars' worth of tyres to collect seventy-five dollars for the British Red Cross- -this is their tag day, you know."

"Roscoe must be very proud," Bella said, and observed the bright glow of pride that appeared in her sister's eyes. "I got the news in San Francisco of Ho-o-la-a's first dividend. Remember when I put a thousand in it at seventy-five cents for poor Abbie's children, and said I'd sell when it went to ten dollars?"

"And everybody laughed at you, and at anybody who bought a share," Martha nodded. "But Roscoe knew. It's selling to-day at twenty- four."

"I sold mine from the steamer by wireless--at twenty even," Bella continued. "And now Abbie's wildly dressmaking. She's going with May and Tootsie to Paris."

"And Carl?" Martha queried.

"Oh, he'll finish Yale all right--"

"Which he would have done anyway, and you KNOW it," Martha charged, lapsing charmingly into twentieth-century slang.

Bella affirmed her guilt of intention of paying the way of her school friend's son through college, and added complacently:

"Just the same it was nicer to have Ho-o-la-a pay for it. In a way, you see, Roscoe is doing it, because it was his judgment I trusted to when I made the investment." She gazed slowly about her, her eyes taking in, not merely the beauty and comfort and repose of all they rested on, but the immensity of beauty and comfort and repose represented by them, scattered in similar oases all over the islands. She sighed pleasantly and observed: "All our husbands have done well by us with what we brought them."

"And happily . . . " Martha agreed, then suspended her utterance with suspicious abruptness.

"And happily, all of us, except Sister Bella," Bella forgivingly completed the thought for her.

"It was too bad, that marriage," Martha murmured, all softness of sympathy. "You were so young. Uncle Robert should never have made you."

"I was only nineteen," Bella nodded. "But it was not George Castner's fault. And look what he, out of she grave, has done for me. Uncle Robert was wise. He knew George had the far-away vision of far ahead, the energy, and the steadiness. He saw, even then, and that's fifty years ago, the value of the Nahala water-rights which nobody else valued then. They thought he was struggling to buy the cattle range. He struggled to buy the future of the water- -and how well he succeeded you know. I'm almost ashamed to think of my income sometimes. No; whatever else, the unhappiness of our marriage was not due to George. I could have lived happily with him, I know, even to this day, had he lived." She shook her head slowly. "No; it was not his fault. Nor anybody's. Not even mine. If it was anybody's fault--" The wistful fondness of her smile took the sting out of what she was about to say. "If it was anybody's fault it was Uncle John's."

"Uncle John's!" Martha cried with sharp surprise. "If it had to be one or the other, I should have said Uncle Robert. But Uncle John!"

Bella smiled with slow positiveness.

"But it was Uncle Robert who made you marry George Castner," her sister urged.

"That is true," Bella nodded corroboration. "But it was not the matter of a husband, but of a horse. I wanted to borrow a horse from Uncle John, and Uncle John said yes. That is how it all happened."

A silence fell, pregnant and cryptic, and, while the voices of the children and the soft mandatory protests of the Asiatic maids drew nearer from the beach, Martha Scandwell felt herself vibrant and tremulous with sudden resolve of daring. She waved the children away.

"Run along, dears, run along, Grandma and Aunt Bella want to talk."

And as the shrill, sweet treble of child voices ebbed away across the lawn, Martha, with scrutiny of the heart, observed the sadness of the lines graven by secret woe for half a century in her sister's face. For nearly fifty years had she watched those lines. She steeled all the melting softness of the Hawaiian of her to break the half-century of silence.

"Bella," she said. "We never know. You never spoke. But we wondered, oh, often and often--"

"And never asked," Bella murmured gratefully.

"But I am asking now, at the last. This is our twilight. Listen to them! Sometimes it almost frightens me to think that they are grandchildren, MY grandchildren--I, who only the other day, it would seem, was as heart-free, leg-free, care-free a girl as ever bestrode a horse, or swam in the big surf, or gathered opihis at low tide, or laughed at a dozen lovers. And here in our twilight let us forget everything save that I am your dear sister as you are mine."

The eyes of both were dewy moist. Bella palpably trembled to utterance.

"We thought it was George Castner," Martha went on; "and we could guess the details. He was a cold man. You were warm Hawaiian. He must have been cruel. Brother Walcott always insisted he must have beaten you--"

"No! No!" Bella broke in. "George Castner was never a brute, a beast. Almost have I wished, often, that he had been. He never laid hand on me. He never raised hand to me. He never raised his voice to me. Never--oh, can you believe it?--do, please, sister, believe it--did we have a high word nor a cross word. But that house of his, of ours, at Nahala, was grey. All the colour of it was grey and cool, and chill, while I was bright with all colours of sun, and earth, and blood, and birth. It was very cold, grey cold, with that cold grey husband of mine at Nahala. You know he was grey, Martha. Grey like those portraits of Emerson we used to see at school. His skin was grey. Sun and weather and all hours in the saddle could never tan it. And he was as grey inside as out.

"And I was only nineteen when Uncle Robert decided on the marriage. How was I to know? Uncle Robert talked to me. He pointed out how the wealth and property of Hawaii was already beginning to pass into the hands of the haoles" (Whites). "The Hawaiian chiefs let their possessions slip away from them. The Hawaiian chiefesses, who married haoles, had their possessions, under the management of their haole husbands, increase prodigiously. He pointed back to the original Grandfather Roger Wilton, who had taken Grandmother Wilton's poor mauka lands and added to them and built up about them the Kilohana Ranch--"

"Even then it was second only to the Parker Ranch," Martha interrupted proudly.

"And he told me that had our father, before he died, been as far-seeing as grandfather, half the then Parker holdings would have been added to Kilohana, making Kilohana first. And he said that never, for ever and ever, would beef be cheaper. And he said that the big future of Hawaii would be in sugar. That was fifty years ago, and he has been more than proved right. And he said that the young haole, George Castner, saw far, and would go far, and that there were many girls of us, and that the Kilohana lands ought by rights to go to the boys, and that if I married George my future was assured in the biggest way.

"I was only nineteen. Just back from the Royal Chief School--that was before our girls went to the States for their education. You were among the first, Sister Martha, who got their education on the mainland. And what did I know of love and lovers, much less of marriage? All women married. It was their business in life. Mother and grandmother, all the way back they had married. It was my business in life to marry George Castner. Uncle Robert said so in his wisdom, and I knew he was very wise. And I went to live with my husband in the grey house at Nahala.

"You remember it. No trees, only the rolling grass lands, the high mountains behind, the sea beneath, and the wind!--the Waimea and Nahala winds, we got them both, and the kona wind as well. Yet little would I have minded them, any more than we minded them at Kilohana, or than they minded them at Mana, had not Nahala itself been so grey, and husband George so grey. We were alone. He was managing Nahala for the Glenns, who had gone back to Scotland. Eighteen hundred a year, plus beef, horses, cowboy service, and the ranch house, was what he received--"

"It was a high salary in those days," Martha said.

"And for George Castner, and the service he gave, it was very cheap," Bella defended. "I lived with him for three years. There was never a morning that he was out of his bed later than half-past four. He was the soul of devotion to his employers. Honest to a penny in his accounts, he gave them full measure and more of his time and energy. Perhaps that was what helped make our life so grey. But listen, Martha. Out of his eighteen hundred, he laid aside sixteen hundred each year. Think of it! The two of us lived on two hundred a year. Luckily he did not drink or smoke. Also, we dressed out of it as well. I made my own dresses. You can imagine them. Outside of the cowboys who chored the firewood, I did the work. I cooked, and baked, and scrubbed--"

"You who had never known anything but servants from the time you were born!" Martha pitied. "Never less than a regiment of them at Kilohana."

"Oh, but it was the bare, naked, pinching meagreness of it!" Bella cried out. "How far I was compelled to make a pound of coffee go! A broom worn down to nothing before a new one was bought! And beef! Fresh beef and jerky, morning, noon, and night! And porridge! Never since have I eaten porridge or any breakfast food."

She arose suddenly and walked a dozen steps away to gaze a moment with unseeing eyes at the colour-lavish reef while she composed herself. And she returned to her seat with the splendid, sure, gracious, high-breasted, noble-headed port of which no out-breeding can ever rob the Hawaiian woman. Very haole was Bella Castner, fair-skinned, fine-textured. Yet, as she returned, the high pose of head, the level-lidded gaze of her long brown eyes under royal arches of eyebrows, the softly set lines of her small mouth that fairly sang sweetness of kisses after sixty-eight years--all made her the very picture of a chiefess of old Hawaii full-bursting through her ampleness of haole blood. Taller she was than her sister Martha, if anything more queenly.

"You know we were notorious as poor feeders," Bella laughed lightly enough. "It was many a mile on either side from Nahala to the next roof. Belated travellers, or storm-bound ones, would, on occasion, stop with us overnight. And you know the lavishness of the big ranches, then and now. How we were the laughing-stock! 'What do we care!' George would say. 'They live to-day and now. Twenty years from now will be our turn, Bella. They will be where they are now, and they will eat out of our hand. We will be compelled to feed them, they will need to be fed, and we will feed them well; for we will be rich, Bella, so rich that I am afraid to tell you. But I know what I know, and you must have faith in me.'

"George was right. Twenty years afterward, though he did not live to see it, my income was a thousand a month. Goodness! I do not know what it is to-day. But I was only nineteen, and I would say to George: 'Now! now! We live now. We may not be alive twenty years from now. I do want a new broom. And there is a third-rate coffee that is only two cents a pound more than the awful stuff we are using. Why couldn't I fry eggs in butter--now? I should dearly love at least one new tablecloth. Our linen! I'm ashamed to put a guest between the sheets, though heaven knows they dare come seldom enough.'

"'Be patient, Bella,' he would reply. 'In a little while, in only a few years, those that scorn to sit at our table now, or sleep between our sheets, will be proud of an invitation--those of them who will not be dead. You remember how Stevens passed out last year--free-living and easy, everybody's friend but his own. The Kohala crowd had to bury him, for he left nothing but debts. Watch the others going the same pace. There's your brother Hal. He can't keep it up and live five years, and he's breaking his uncles' hearts. And there's Prince Lilolilo. Dashes by me with half a hundred mounted, able-bodied, roystering kanakas in his train who would be better at hard work and looking after their future, for he will never be king of Hawaii. He will not live to be king of Hawaii.'

"George was right. Brother Hal died. So did Prince Lilolilo. But George was not ALL right. He, who neither drank nor smoked, who never wasted the weight of his arms in an embrace, nor the touch of his lips a second longer than the most perfunctory of kisses, who was invariably up before cockcrow and asleep ere the kerosene lamp had a tenth emptied itself, and who never thought to die, was dead even more quickly than Brother Hal and Prince Lilolilo.

"'Be patient, Bella,' Uncle Robert would say to me. 'George Castner is a coming man. I have chosen well for you. Your hardships now are the hardships on the way to the promised land. Not always will the Hawaiians rule in Hawaii. Just as they let their wealth slip out of their hands, so will their rule slip out of their hands. Political power and the land always go together. There will be great changes, revolutions no one knows how many nor of what sort, save that in the end the haole will possess the land and the rule. And in that day you may well be first lady of

Hawaii, just as surely as George Castner will be ruler of Hawaii. It is written in the books. It is ever so where the haole conflicts with the easier races. I, your Uncle Robert, who am half-Hawaiian and half-haole, know whereof I speak. Be patient, Bella, be patient.'

"'Dear Bella,' Uncle John would say; and I knew his heart was tender for me. Thank God, he never told me to be patient. He knew. He was very wise. He was warm human, and, therefore, wiser than Uncle Robert and George Castner, who sought the thing, not the spirit, who kept records in ledgers rather than numbers of heart- beats breast to breast, who added columns of figures rather than remembered embraces and endearments of look and speech and touch. 'Dear Bella,' Uncle John would say. He knew. You have heard always how he was the lover of the Princess Naomi. He was a true lover. He loved but the once. After her death they said he was eccentric. He was. He was the one lover, once and always. Remember that taboo inner room of his at Kilohana that we entered only after his death and found it his shrine to her. 'Dear Bella,' it was all he ever said to me, but I knew he knew.

"And I was nineteen, and sun-warm Hawaiian in spite of my three- quarters haole blood, and I knew nothing save my girlhood splendours at Kilohana and my Honolulu education at the Royal Chief School, and my grey husband at Nahala with his grey preachments and practices of sobriety and thrift, and those two childless uncles of mine, the one with far, cold vision, the other the broken-hearted, for-ever-dreaming lover of a dead princess.

"Think of that grey house! I, who had known the ease and the delights and the ever-laughing joys of Kilohana, and of the Parkers at old Mana, and of Puuwaawaa! You remember. We did live in feudal spaciousness in those days. Would you, can you, believe it, Martha--at Nahala the only sewing machine I had was one of those the early missionaries brought, a tiny, crazy thing that one cranked around by hand!

"Robert and John had each given Husband George five thousand dollars at my marriage. But he had asked for it to be kept secret. Only the four of us knew. And while I sewed my cheap holokus on that crazy machine, he bought land with the money--the upper Nahala lands, you know--a bit at a time, each purchase a hard-driven bargain, his face the very face of poverty. To-day the Nahala Ditch alone pays me forty thousand a year.

"But was it worth it? I starved. If only once, madly, he had crushed me in his arms! If only once he could have lingered with me five minutes from his own business or from his fidelity to his employers! Sometimes I could have screamed, or showered the eternal bowl of hot porridge into his face, or smashed the sewing machine upon the floor and danced a hula on it, just to make him burst out and lose his temper and be human, be a brute, be a man of some sort instead of a grey, frozen demi-god."

Bella's tragic expression vanished, and she laughed outright in sheer genuineness of mirthful recollection.

"And when I was in such moods he would gravely look me over, gravely feel my pulse, examine my tongue, gravely dose me with castor oil, and gravely put me to bed early with hot stove-lids, and assure me that I'd feel better in the morning. Early to bed! Our wildest sitting up was nine o'clock. Eight o'clock was our regular bed-time. It saved kerosene. We did not eat dinner at Nahala--remember the great table at Kilohana where we did have dinner? But Husband George and I had supper. And then he would sit close to the lamp on one side the table and read old borrowed magazines for an hour, while I sat on the other side and darned his socks and underclothing. He always wore such cheap, shoddy stuff. And when he went to bed, I went to bed. No wastage of kerosene with only one to benefit by it. And he went to bed always the same way, winding up his watch, entering the day's weather in his diary, and taking off his shoes, right foot first invariably, left foot second, and placing them just so, side by side, on the floor, at the foot of the bed, on his side.

"He was the cleanest man I ever knew. He never wore the same undergarment a second time. I did the washing. He was so clean it hurt. He shaved twice a day. He used more water on his body than any kanaka. He did more work than any two haoles. And he saw the future of the Nahala water."

"And he made you wealthy, but did not make you happy," Martha observed.

Bella sighed and nodded.

"What is wealth after all, Sister Martha? My new Pierce-Arrow came down on the steamer with me. My third in two years. But oh, all the Pierce-Arrows and all the incomes in the world compared with a lover!--the one lover, the one mate, to be married to, to toil beside and suffer and joy beside, the one male man lover husband . . . "

Her voice trailed off, and the sisters sat in soft silence while an ancient crone, staff in hand, twisted, doubled, and shrunken under a hundred years of living, hobbled across the lawn to them. Her eyes, withered to scarcely more than peepholes, were sharp as a mongoose's, and at Bella's feet she first sank down, in pure Hawaiian mumbling and chanting a toothless mele of Bella and Bella's ancestry and adding to it an extemporized welcome back to Hawaii after her absence across the great sea to California. And while she chanted her mele, the old crone's shrewd fingers lomied or massaged Bella's silk-stockinged legs from ankle and calf to knee and thigh.

Both Bella's and Martha's eyes were luminous-moist, as the old retainer repeated the lomi and the mele to Martha, and as they talked with her in the ancient tongue and asked the immemorial questions about her health and age and great-great-grandchildren-- she who had lomied them as babies in the great house at Kilohana, as her ancestresses had lomied their ancestresses back through the unnumbered generations. The brief duty visit over, Martha arose and accompanied her back to the bungalow, putting money into her hand, commanding proud and beautiful Japanese housemaids to wait upon the dilapidated aborigine with poi, which is compounded of the roots of the water lily, with iamaka, which is raw fish, and with pounded kukui nut and limu, which latter is seawood tender to the toothless, digestible and savoury. It was the old feudal tie, the faithfulness of the commoner to the chief, the responsibility of the chief to the commoner; and Martha, three-quarters haole with the Anglo-Saxon blood of New England, was four-quarters Hawaiian in her remembrance and observance of the well-nigh vanished customs of old days.

As she came back across the lawn to the hau tree, Bella's eyes dwelt upon the moving authenticity of her and of the blood of her, and embraced her and loved her. Shorter than Bella was Martha, a trifle, but the merest trifle, less queenly of port; but beautifully and generously proportioned, mellowed rather than dismantled by years, her Polynesian chiefess figure eloquent and glorious under the satisfying lines of a half-fitting, grandly sweeping, black-silk holoku trimmed with black lace more costly than a Paris gown.

And as both sisters resumed their talk, an observer would have noted the striking resemblance of their pure, straight profiles, of their broad cheek-bones, of their wide and lofty foreheads, of their iron-grey abundance of hair, of their sweet-lipped mouths set with the carriage of decades of assured and accomplished pride, and of their lovely slender eye-rows arched over equally lovely long brown eyes. The hands of both of them, little altered or defaced by age, were wonderful in their slender, tapering finger-tips, love-lomied and love-formed while they were babies by old Hawaiian women like to the one even then eating poi and iamaka and limu in the house.

"I had a year of it," Bella resumed, "and, do you know, things were beginning to come right. I was beginning to draw to Husband George. Women are so made, I was such a woman at any rate. For he was good. He was just. All the old sterling Puritan virtues were his. I was coming to draw to him, to like him, almost, might I say, to love him. And had not Uncle John loaned me that horse, I know that I would have truly loved him and have lived ever happily with him--in a quiet sort of way, of course.

"You see, I knew nothing else, nothing different, nothing better in the way of men. I came gladly to look across the table at him while he read in the brief interval between supper and bed, gladly to listen for and to catch the beat of his horse's hoofs coming home at night from his endless riding over the ranch. And his scant praise was praise indeed, that made me tingle with happiness- -yes, Sister Martha, I knew what it was to blush under his precise, just praise for the things I had done right or correctly.

"And all would have been well for the rest of our lives together, except that he had to take steamer to Honolulu. It was business. He was to be gone two weeks or longer, first, for the Glenns in ranch affairs, and next for himself, to arrange the purchase of still more of the upper Nahala lands. Do you know! he bought lots of the wilder and up-and-down lands, worthless for aught save water, and the very heart of the watershed, for as low as five and ten cents an acre. And he suggested I needed a change. I wanted to go with him to Honolulu. But, with an eye to expense, he decided Kilohana for me. Not only would it cost him nothing for me to visit at the old home, but he saved the price of the poor food I should have eaten had I remained alone at Nahala, which meant the purchase price of more Nahala acreage. And at Kilohana Uncle John said yes, and loaned me the horse.

"Oh, it was like heaven, getting back, those first several days. It was difficult to believe at first that there was so much food in all the world. The enormous wastage of the kitchen appalled me. I saw waste everywhere, so well trained had I been by Husband George. Why, out in the servants' quarters the aged relatives and most distant hangers-on of the servants fed better than George and I ever fed. You remember our Kilohana way, same as the Parker way, a bullock killed for every meal, fresh fish by runners from the ponds of Waipio and Kiholo, the best and rarest at all times of everything . . .

"And love, our family way of loving! You know what Uncle John was. And Brother Walcott was there, and Brother Edward, and all the younger sisters save you and Sally away at school. And Aunt Elizabeth, and Aunt Janet with her husband and all her children on a visit. It was arms around, and perpetual endearings, and all that I had missed for a weary twelvemonth. I was thirsty for it. I was like a survivor from the open boat falling down on the sand and lapping the fresh bubbling springs at the roots of the palms.

"And THEY came, riding up from Kawaihae, where they had landed from the royal yacht, the whole glorious cavalcade of them, two by two, flower-garlanded, young and happy, gay, on Parker Ranch horses, thirty of them in the party, a hundred Parker Ranch cowboys and as many more of their own retainers--a royal progress. It was Princess Lihue's progress, of course, she flaming and passing as we all knew with the dreadful tuberculosis; but with her were her nephews, Prince Lilolilo, hailed everywhere as the next king, and his brothers, Prince Kahekili and Prince Kamalau. And with the Princess was Ella Higginsworth, who rightly claimed higher chief blood lines through the Kauai descent than belonged to the reigning family, and Dora Niles, and Emily Lowcroft, and . . . oh, why enumerate them all! Ella Higginsworth and I had been room-mates at the Royal Chief School. And there was a great resting time for an hour--no luau, for the luau awaited them at the Parkers'--but beer and stronger drinks for the men, and lemonade, and oranges, and refreshing watermelon for the women.

"And it was arms around with Ella Higginsworth and me, and the Princess, who remembered me, and all the other girls and women, and Ella spoke to the Princess, and the Princess herself invited me to the progress, joining them at Mana whence they would depart two days later. And I was mad, mad with it all--I, from a twelvemonth of imprisonment at grey Nahala. And I was nineteen yet, just turning twenty within the week.

"Oh, I had not thought of what was to happen. So occupied was I with the women that I did not see Lilolilo, except at a distance, bulking large and tall above the other men. But I had never been on a progress. I had seen them entertained at Kilohana and Mana, but I had been too young to be invited along, and after that it had been school and marriage. I knew what it would be like--two weeks of paradise, and little enough for another twelve months at Nahala.

"And I asked Uncle John to lend me a horse, which meant three horses of course--one mounted cowboy and a pack horse to accompany me. No roads then. No automobiles. And the horse for myself! It was Hilo. You don't remember him. You were away at school then, and before you came home, the following year, he'd broken his back and his rider's neck wild-cattle-roping up Mauna Kea. You heard about it--that young American naval officer."

"Lieutenant Bowsfield," Martha nodded.

"But Hilo! I was the first woman on his back. He was a three- year-old, almost a four-year, and just broken. So black and in such a vigour of coat that the high lights on him clad him in shimmering silver. He was the biggest riding animal on the ranch, descended from the King's Sparklingdow with a range mare for dam, and roped wild only two weeks before. I never have seen so beautiful a horse. He had the round, deep-chested, big-hearted, well-coupled body of the ideal mountain pony, and his head and neck were true thoroughbred, slender, yet full, with lovely alert ears not too small to be vicious nor too large to be stubborn mulish. And his legs and feet were lovely too, unblemished, sure and firm, with long springy pasterns that made him a wonder of ease under the saddle."

"I remember hearing Prince Lilolilo tell Uncle John that you were the best woman rider in all Hawaii," Martha interrupted to say. "That was two years afterward when I was back from school and while you were still living at Nahala."

"Lilolilo said that!" Bella cried. Almost as with a blush, her long, brown eyes were illumined, as she bridged the years to her lover near half a century dead and dust. With the gentleness of modesty so innate in the women of Hawaii, she covered her spontaneous exposure of her heart with added panegyric of Hilo.

"Oh, when he ran with me up the long-grass slopes, and down the long-grass slopes, it was like hurdling in a dream, for he cleared the grass at every bound, leaping like a deer, a rabbit, or a fox- terrier--you know how they do. And cut up, and prance, and high life! He was a mount for a general, for a Napoleon or a Kitchener. And he had, not a wicked eye, but, oh, such a roguish eye, intelligent and looking as if it cherished a joke behind and wanted to laugh or to perpetrate it. And I asked Uncle John for Hilo. And Uncle John looked at me, and I looked at him; and, though he did not say it, I knew he was FEELING 'Dear Bella,' and I knew, somewhere in his seeing of me, was all his vision of the Princess Naomi. And Uncle John said yes. That is how it happened.

"But he insisted that I should try Hilo out--myself, rather--at private rehearsal. He was a handful, a glorious handful. But not vicious, not malicious. He got away from me over and over again, but I never let him know. I was not afraid, and that helped me keep always a feel of him that prevented him from thinking that he was even a jump ahead of me.

"I have often wondered if Uncle John dreamed of what possibly might happen. I know I had no thought of it myself, that day I rode across and joined the Princess at Mana. Never was there such festal time. You know the grand way the old Parkers had of entertaining. The pig-sticking and wild-cattle-shooting, the horse-breaking and the branding. The servants' quarters overflowing. Parker cowboys in from everywhere. And all the girls from Waimea up, and the girls from Waipio, and Honokaa, and Paauilo--I can see them yet, sitting in long rows on top the stone walls of the breaking pen and making leis" (flower garlands) "for their cowboy lovers. And the nights, the perfumed nights, the chanting of the meles and the dancing of the hulas, and the big Mana grounds with lovers everywhere strolling two by two under the trees.

"And the Prince . . . " Bella paused, and for a long minute her small fine teeth, still perfect, showed deep in her underlip as she sought and won control and sent her gaze vacantly out across the far blue horizon. As she relaxed, her eyes came back to her sister.

"He was a prince, Martha. You saw him at Kilohana before . . . after you came home from seminary. He filled the eyes of any woman, yes, and of any man. Twenty-five he was, in all-glorious ripeness of man, great and princely in body as he was great and princely in spirit. No matter how wild the fun, how reckless mad the sport, he never seemed to forget that he was royal, and that all his forebears had been high chiefs even to that first one they sang in the genealogies, who had navigated his double-canoes to Tahiti and Raiatea and back again. He was gracious, sweet, kindly comradely, all friendliness--and severe, and stern, and harsh, if he were crossed too grievously. It is hard to express what I mean. He was all man, man, man, and he was all prince, with a strain of the merry boy in him, and the iron in him that would have made him a good and strong king of Hawaii had he come to the throne.

"I can see him yet, as I saw him that first day and touched his hand and talked with him . . . few words and bashful, and anything but a year-long married woman to a grey haole at grey Nahala. Half a century ago it was, that meeting--you remember how our young men then dressed in white shoes and trousers, white silk shirts, with slashed around the middle the gorgeously colourful Spanish sashes-- and for half a century that picture of him has not faded in my heart. He was the centre of a group on the lawn, and I was being brought by Ella Higginsworth to be presented. The Princess Lihue had just called some teasing chaff to her which had made her halt to respond and left me halted a pace in front of her.

"His glance chanced to light on me, alone there, perturbed, embarrassed. Oh, how I see him!--his head thrown back a little, with that high, bright, imperious, and utterly care-free poise that was so usual of him. Our eyes met. His head bent forward, or straightened to me, I don't know what happened. Did he command? Did I obey? I do not know. I know only that I was good to look upon, crowned with fragrant maile, clad in Princess Naomi's wonderful holoku loaned me by Uncle John from his taboo room; and I know that I advanced alone to him across the Mana lawn, and that he stepped forth from those about him to meet me half-way. We came to each other across the grass, unattended, as if we were coming to each other across our lives.

"--Was I very beautiful, Sister Martha, when I was young? I do not know. I don't know. But in that moment, with all his beauty and truly royal-manness crossing to me and penetrating to the heart of me, I felt a sudden sense of beauty in myself--how shall I say? as if in him and from him perfection were engendered and conjured within myself.

"No word was spoken. But, oh, I know I raised my face in frank answer to the thunder and trumpets of the message unspoken, and that, had it been death for that one look and that one moment I could not have refrained from the gift of myself that must have been in my face and eyes, in the very body of me that breathed so high.

"Was I beautiful, very beautiful, Martha, when I was nineteen, just turning into twenty?"

And Martha, three-score and four, looked upon Bella, three-score and eight, and nodded genuine affirmation, and to herself added the appreciation of the instant in what she beheld-- Bella's neck, still full and shapely, longer than the ordinary Hawaiian woman's neck, a pillar that carried regally her high-cheeked, high-browed, high chiefess face and head; Bella's hair, high-piled, intact, sparkling the silver of the years, ringleted still and contrasting definitely and sharply with her clean, slim, black brows and deep brown eyes. And Martha's glance, in modest overwhelming of modesty by what she saw, dropped down the splendid breast of her and generously true lines of body to the feet, silken clad, high-heeled-slippered, small, plump, with an almost Spanish arch and faultlessness of instep.

"When one is young, the one young time!" Bella laughed. "Lilolilo was a prince. I came to know his every feature and their every phase . . . afterward, in our wonder days and nights by the singing waters, by the slumber-drowsy surfs, and on the mountain ways. I knew his fine, brave eyes, with their straight, black brows, the nose of him that was assuredly a Kamehameha nose, and the last, least, lovable curve of his mouth. There is no mouth more beautiful than the Hawaiian, Martha.

"And his body. He was a king of athletes, from his wicked, wayward hair to his ankles of bronzed steel. Just the other day I heard one of the Wilder grandsons referred to as 'The Prince of Harvard.' Mercy! What would they, what could they have called my Lilolilo could they have matched him against this Wilder lad and all his team at Harvard!"

Bella ceased and breathed deeply, the while she clasped her fine small hands in her ample silken lap. But her pink fairness blushed faintly through her skin and warmed her eyes as she relived her prince-days.

"Well--you have guessed?" Bella said, with defiant shrug of shoulders and a straight gaze into her sister's eyes. "We rode out from gay Mana and continued the gay progress--down the lava trails to Kiholo to the swimming and the fishing and the feasting and the sleeping in the warm sand under the palms; and up to Puuwaawaa, and more pig-sticking, and roping and driving, and wild mutton from the upper pasture-lands; and on through Kona, now mauka" (mountainward), "now down to the King's palace at Kailua, and to the swimming at Keauhou, and to Kealakekua Bay, and Napoopoo and Honaunau. And everywhere the people turning out, in their hands gifts of flowers, and fruit, and fish, and pig, in their hearts love and song, their heads bowed in obeisance to the royal ones while their lips ejaculated exclamations of amazement or chanted meles of old and unforgotten days.

"What would you, Sister Martha? You know what we Hawaiians are. You know what we were half a hundred years ago. Lilolilo was wonderful. I was reckless. Lilolilo of himself could make any woman reckless. I was twice reckless, for I had cold, grey Nahala to spur me on. I knew. I had never a doubt. Never a hope. Divorces in those days were undreamed. The wife of George Castner could never be queen of Hawaii, even if Uncle Robert's prophesied revolutions were delayed, and if Lilolilo himself became king. But I never thought of the throne. What I wanted would have been the queendom of being Lilolilo's wife and mate. But I made no mistake. What was impossible was impossible, and I dreamed no false dream.

"It was the very atmosphere of love. And Lilolilo was a lover. I was for ever crowned with leis by him, and he had his runners bring me leis all the way from the rose-gardens of Mana--you remember them; fifty miles across the lava and the ranges, dewy fresh as the moment they were plucked, in their jewel-cases of banana bark; yard-long they were, the tiny pink buds like threaded beads of Neapolitan coral. And at the luaus" (feasts) the for ever never- ending luaus, I must be seated on Lilolilo's Makaloa mat, the Prince's mat, his alone and taboo to any lesser mortal save by his own condescension and desire. And I must dip my fingers into his own pa wai holoi" (finger-bowl) "where scented flower petals floated in the warm water. Yes, and careless that all should see his extended favour, I must dip into his pa paakai for my pinches of red salt, and limu, and kukui nut and chili pepper; and into his ipu kai" (fish sauce dish) "of kou wood that the great Kamehameha himself had eaten from on many a similar progress. And it was the same for special delicacies that were for Lilolilo and the Princess alone--for his nelu, and the ake, and the palu, and the alaala. And his kahilis were waved over me, and his attendants were mine, and he was mine; and from my flower-crowned hair to my happy feet I was a woman loved."

Once again Bella's small teeth pressed into her underlip, as she gazed vacantly seaward and won control of herself and her memories.

"It was on, and on, through all Kona, and all Kau, from Hoopuloa and Kapua to Honuapo and Punaluu, a life-time of living compressed into two short weeks. A flower blooms but once. That was my time of bloom--Lilolilo beside me, myself on my wonderful Hilo, a queen, not of Hawaii, but of Lilolilo and Love. He said I was a bubble of colour and beauty on the black back of Leviathan; that I was a fragile dewdrop on the smoking crest of a lava flow; that I was a rainbow riding the thunder cloud . . . "

Bella paused for a moment.

"I shall tell you no more of what he said to me," she declared gravely; "save that the things he said were fire of love and essence of beauty, and that he composed hulas to me, and sang them to me, before all, of nights under the stars as we lay on our mats at the feasting; and I on the Makaloa mat of Lilolilo.

"And it was on to Kilauea--the dream so near its ending; and of course we tossed into the pit of sea-surging lava our offerings to the Fire-Goddess of maile leis and of fish and hard poi wrapped moist in the ti leaves. And we continued down through old Puna, and feasted and danced and sang at Kohoualea and Kamaili and Opihikao, and swam in the clear, sweet-water pools of Kalapana. And in the end came to Hilo by the sea.

"It was the end. We had never spoken. It was the end recognized and unmentioned. The yacht waited. We were days late. Honolulu called, and the news was that the King had gone particularly pupule" (insane), "that there were Catholic and Protestant missionary plottings, and that trouble with France was brewing. As they had landed at Kawaihae two weeks before with laughter and flowers and song, so they departed from Hilo. It was a merry parting, full of fun and frolic and a thousand last messages and reminders and jokes. The anchor was broken out to a song of farewell from Lilolilo's singing boys on the quarterdeck, while we, in the big canoes and whaleboats, saw the first breeze fill the vessel's sails and the distance begin to widen.

"Through all the confusion and excitement, Lilolilo, at the rail, who must say last farewells and quip last jokes to many, looked squarely down at me. On his head he wore my ilima lei, which I had made for him and placed there. And into the canoes, to the favoured ones, they on the yacht began tossing their many leis. I had no expectancy of hope . . . And yet I hoped, in a small wistful way that I know did not show in my face, which was as proud and merry as any there. But Lilolilo did what I knew he would do, what I had known from the first he would do. Still looking me squarely and honestly in the eyes, he took my beautiful ilima lei from his head and tore it across. I saw his lips shape, but not utter aloud, the single word pau" (finish). "Still looking at me, he broke both parts of the lei in two again and tossed the deliberate fragments, not to me, but down overside into the widening water. Pau. It was finished . . . "

For a long space Bella's vacant gaze rested on the sea horizon. Martha ventured no mere voice expression of the sympathy that moistened her own eyes.

"And I rode on that day, up the old bad trail along the Hamakua coast," Bella resumed, with a voice at first singularly dry and harsh. "That first day was not so hard. I was numb. I was too full with the wonder of all I had to forget to know that I had to forget it. I spent the night at Laupahoehoe. Do you know, I had expected a sleepless night. Instead, weary from the saddle, still numb, I slept the night through as if I had been dead.

"But the next day, in driving wind and drenching rain! How it blew and poured! The trail was really impassable. Again and again our horses went down. At fist the cowboy Uncle John had loaned me with the horses protested, then he followed stolidly in the rear, shaking his head, and, I know, muttering over and over that I was pupule. The pack horse was abandoned at Kukuihaele. We almost swam up Mud Lane in a river of mud. At Waimea the cowboy had to exchange for a fresh mount. But Hilo lasted through. From daybreak till midnight I was in the saddle, till Uncle John, at Kilohana, took me off my horse, in his arms, and carried me in, and routed the women from their beds to undress me and lomi me, while he plied me with hot toddies and drugged me to sleep and forgetfulness. I know I must have babbled and raved. Uncle John must have guessed. But never to another, nor even to me, did he ever breathe a whisper. Whatever he guessed he locked away in the taboo room of Naomi.

"I do have fleeting memories of some of that day, all a broken- hearted mad rage against fate--of my hair down and whipped wet and stinging about me in the driving rain; of endless tears of weeping contributed to the general deluge, of passionate outbursts and resentments against a world all twisted and wrong, of beatings of my hands upon my saddle pommel, of asperities to my Kilohana cowboy, of spurs into the ribs of poor magnificent Hilo, with a prayer on my lips, bursting out from my heart, that the spurs would so madden him as to make him rear and fall on me and crush my body for ever out of all beauty for man, or topple me off the trail and finish me at the foot of the palis" (precipices), "writing pau at the end of my name as final as the unuttered pau on Lilolilo's lips when he tore across my ilima lei and dropped it in the sea. . . .

"Husband George was delayed in Honolulu. When he came back to Nahala I was there waiting for him. And solemnly he embraced me, perfunctorily kissed my lips, gravely examined my tongue, decried my looks and state of health, and sent me to bed with hot stove- lids and a dosage of castor oil. Like entering into the machinery of a clock and becoming one of the cogs or wheels, inevitably and remorselessly turning around and around, so I entered back into the grey life of Nahala. Out of bed was Husband George at half after four every morning, and out of the house and astride his horse at five. There was the eternal porridge, and the horrible cheap coffee, and the fresh beef and jerky. I cooked, and baked, and scrubbed. I ground around the crazy hand sewing machine and made my cheap holokus. Night after night, through the endless centuries of two years more, I sat across the table from him until eight o'clock, mending his cheap socks and shoddy underwear, while he read the years' old borrowed magazines he was too thrifty to subscribe to. And then it was bed-time--kerosene must be economized--and he wound his watch, entered the weather in his diary, and took off his shoes, the right shoe first, and placed them, just so, side by side, at the foot of the bed on his side.

"But there was no more of my drawing to Husband George, as had been the promise ere the Princess Lihue invited me on the progress and Uncle John loaned me the horse. You see, Sister Martha, nothing would have happened had Uncle John refused me the horse. But I had known love, and I had known Lilolilo; and what chance, after that, had Husband George to win from me heart of esteem or affection? And for two years, at Nahala, I was a dead woman who somehow walked and talked, and baked and scrubbed, and mended socks and saved kerosene. The doctors said it was the shoddy underwear that did for him, pursuing as always the high-mountain Nahala waters in the drenching storms of midwinter.

"When he died, I was not sad. I had been sad too long already. Nor was I glad. Gladness had died at Hilo when Lilolilo dropped my ilima lei into the sea and my feet were never happy again. Lilolilo passed within a month after Husband George. I had never seen him since the parting at Hilo. La, la, suitors a many have I had since; but I was like Uncle John. Mating for me was but once. Uncle John had his Naomi room at Kilohana. I have had my Lilolilo room for fifty years in my heart. You are the first, Sister Martha, whom I have permitted to enter that room . . ."

A machine swung the circle of the drive, and from it, across the lawn, approached the husband of Martha. Erect, slender, grey- haired, of graceful military bearing, Roscoe Scandwell was a member of the "Big Five," which, by the interlocking of interests, determined the destinies of all Hawaii. Himself pure haole, New England born, he kissed Bella first, arms around, full-hearty, in the Hawaiian way. His alert eye told him that there had been a woman talk, and, despite the signs of all generousness of emotion, that all was well and placid in the twilight wisdom that was theirs.

"Elsie and the younglings are coming--just got a wireless from their steamer," he announced, after he had kissed his wife. "And they'll be spending several days with us before they go on to Maui."

"I was going to put you in the Rose Room, Sister Bella," Martha Scandwell planned aloud. "But it will be better for her and the children and the nurses and everything there, so you shall have Queen Emma's Room."

"I had it last time, and I prefer it," Bella said.

Roscoe Scandwell, himself well taught of Hawaiian love and love- ways, erect, slender, dignified, between the two nobly proportioned women, an arm around each of their sumptuous waists, proceeded with them toward the house.

WAIKIKI, HAWAII.
June 6, 1916

The Bones of Kahekili

From over the lofty Koolau Mountains, vagrant wisps of the trade wind drifted, faintly swaying the great, unwhipped banana leaves, rustling the palms, and fluttering and setting up a whispering among the lace-leaved algaroba trees. Only intermittently did the atmosphere so breathe--for breathing it was, the suspiring of the languid, Hawaiian afternoon. In the intervals between the soft breathings, the air grew heavy and balmy with the perfume of flowers and the exhalations of fat, living soil.

Of humans about the low bungalow-like house, there were many; but one only of them slept. The rest were on the tense tiptoes of silence. At the rear of the house a tiny babe piped up a thin blatting wail that the quickly thrust breast could not appease. The mother, a slender hapa-haole (half-white), clad in a loose- flowing holoku of white muslin, hastened away swiftly among the banana and papaia trees to remove the babe's noise by distance. Other women, hapa-haole and full native, watched her anxiously as she fled.

At the front of the house, on the grass, squatted a score of Hawaiians. Well-muscled, broad-shouldered, they were all strapping men. Brown-skinned, with luminous brown eyes and black, their features large and regular, they showed all the signs of being as good-natured, merry-hearted, and soft-tempered as the climate. To all of which a seeming contradiction was given by the ferociousness of their accoutrement. Into the tops of their rough leather leggings were thrust long knives, the handles projecting. On their heels were huge-rowelled Spanish spurs. They had the appearance of banditti, save for the incongruous wreaths of flowers and fragrant maile that encircled the crowns of their flopping cowboy hats. One of them, deliciously and roguishly handsome as a faun, with the eyes of a faun, wore a flaming double-hibiscus bloom coquettishly tucked over his ear. Above them, casting a shelter of shade from the sun, grew a wide-spreading canopy of Ponciana regia, itself a flame of blossoms, out of each of which sprang pom-poms of feathery stamens. From far off, muffled by distance, came the faint stamping of their tethered horses. The eyes of all were intently fixed upon the solitary sleeper who lay on his back on a lauhala mat a hundred feet away under the monkey-pod trees.

Large as were the Hawaiian cowboys, the sleeper was larger. Also, as his snow-white hair and beard attested, he was much older. The thickness of his wrist and the greatness of his fingers made authentic the mighty frame of him hidden under loose dungaree pants and cotton shirt, buttonless, open from midriff to Adam's apple, exposing a chest matted with a thatch of hair as white as that of his head and face. The depth and breadth of that chest, its resilience, and its relaxed and plastic muscles, tokened the knotty strength that still resided in him. Further, no bronze and beat of sun and wind availed to hide the testimony of his skin that he was all haole--a white man.

On his back, his great white beard, thrust skyward, untrimmed of barbers, stiffened and subsided with every breath, while with the outblow of every exhalation the white moustache erected perpendicularly like the quills of a porcupine and subsided with each intake. A young girl of fourteen, clad only in a single shift, or muumuu, herself a grand-daughter of the sleeper, crouched beside him and with a feathered fly-flapper brushed away the flies. In her face were depicted solicitude, and nervousness, and awe, as if she attended on a god.

And truly, Hardman Pool, the sleeping whiskery one, was to her, and to many and sundry, a god--a source of life, a source of food, a fount of wisdom, a giver of law, a smiling beneficence, a blackness of thunder and punishment--in short, a man-master whose record was fourteen living and adult sons and daughters, six great- grandchildren, and more grandchildren than could he in his most lucid moments enumerate.

Fifty-one years before, he had landed from an open boat at Laupahoehoe on the windward coast of Hawaii. The boat was the one surviving one of the whaler Black Prince of New Bedford. Himself New Bedford born, twenty years of age, by virtue of his driving strength and ability he had served as second mate on the lost whaleship. Coming to Honolulu and casting about for himself, he had first married Kalama Mamaiopili, next acted as pilot of Honolulu Harbour, after that started a saloon and boarding house, and, finally, on the death of Kalama's father, engaged in cattle ranching on the broad pasture lands she had inherited.

For over half a century he had lived with the Hawaiians, and it was conceded that he knew their language better than did most of them. By marrying Kalama, he had married not merely her land, but her own chief rank, and the fealty owed by the commoners to her by virtue of her genealogy was also accorded him. In addition, he possessed of himself all the natural attributes of chiefship: the gigantic stature, the fearlessness, the pride; and the high hot temper that could brook no impudence nor insult, that could be neither bullied nor awed by any utmost magnificence of power that walked on two legs, and that could compel service of lesser humans, not by any ignoble purchase by bargaining, but by an unspoken but expected condescending of largesse. He knew his Hawaiians from the outside and the in, knew them better than themselves, their Polynesian circumlocutions, faiths, customs, and mysteries.

And at seventy-one, after a morning in the saddle over the ranges that began at four o'clock, he lay under the monkey-pods in his customary and sacred siesta that no retainer dared to break, nor would dare permit any equal of the great one to break. Only to the King was such a right accorded, and, as the King had early learned, to break Hardman Pool's siesta was to gain awake a very irritable and grumpy Hardman Pool who would talk straight from the shoulder and say unpleasant but true things that no king would care to hear.

The sun blazed down. The horses stamped remotely. The fading trade-wind wisps sighed and rustled between longer intervals of quiescence. The perfume grew heavier. The woman brought back the babe, quiet again, to the rear of the house. The monkey-pods folded their leaves and swooned to a siesta of their own in the soft air above the sleeper. The girl, breathless as ever from the enormous solemnity of her task, still brushed the flies away; and the score of cowboys still intently and silently watched.

Hardman Pool awoke. The next out-breath, expected of the long rhythm, did not take place. Neither did the white, long moustache rise up. Instead, the cheeks, under the whiskers, puffed; the eyelids lifted, exposing blue eyes, choleric and fully and immediately conscious; the right hand went out to the half-smoked pipe beside him, while the left hand reached the matches.

"Get me my gin and milk," he ordered, in Hawaiian, of the little maid, who had been startled into a tremble by his awaking.

He lighted the pipe, but gave no sign of awareness of the presence of his waiting retainers until the tumbler of gin and milk had been brought and drunk.

"Well?" he demanded abruptly, and in the pause, while twenty faces wreathed in smiles and twenty pairs of dark eyes glowed luminously with well-wishing pleasure, he wiped the lingering drops of gin and milk from his hairy lips. "What are you hanging around for? What do you want? Come over here."

Twenty giants, most of them young, uprose and with a great clanking and jangling of spurs and spur-chains strode over to him. They grouped before him in a semicircle, trying bashfully to wedge their shoulders, one behind another's, their faces a-grin and apologetic, and at the same time expressing a casual and unconscious democraticness. In truth, to them Hardman

Pool was more than mere chief. He was elder brother, or father, or patriarch; and to all of them he was related, in one way or another, according to Hawaiian custom, through his wife and through the many marriages of his children and grandchildren. His slightest frown might perturb them, his anger terrify them, his command compel them to certain death; yet, on the other hand, not one of them would have dreamed of addressing him otherwise than intimately by his first name, which name, "Hardman," was transmuted by their tongues into Kanaka Oolea.

At a nod from him, the semicircle seated itself on the manienie grass, and with further deprecatory smiles waited his pleasure.

"What do you want?" demanded, in Hawaiian, with a brusqueness and sternness they knew were put on.

They smiled more broadly, and deliciously squirmed their broad shoulders and great torsos with the appeasingness of so many wriggling puppies. Hardman Pool singled out one of them.

"Well, Iliiopoi, what do YOU want?"

"Ten dollars, Kanaka Oolea."

"Ten dollars!" Pool cried, in apparent shock at mention of so vast a sum. "Does it mean you are going to take a second wife? Remember the missionary teaching. One wife at a time, Iliiopoi; one wife at a time. For he who entertains a plurality of wives will surely go to hell."

Giggles and flashings of laughing eyes from all greeted the joke.

"No, Kanaka Oolea," came the reply. "The devil knows I am hard put to get kow-kow for one wife and her several relations."

"Kow-kow?" Pool repeated the Chinese-introduced word for food which the Hawaiians had come to substitute for their own paina. "Didn't you boys get kow-kow here this noon?"

"Yes, Kanaka Oolea," volunteered an old, withered native who had just joined the group from the direction of the house. "All of them had kow-kow in the kitchen, and plenty of it. They ate like lost horses brought down from the lava."

"And what do you want, Kumuhana?" Pool diverted to the old one, at the same time motioning to the little maid to flap flies from the other side of him.

"Twelve dollars," said Kumuhana. "I want to buy a Jackass and a second-hand saddle and bridle. I am growing too old for my legs to carry me in walking."

"You wait," his haole lord commanded. "I will talk with you about the matter, and about other things of importance, when I am finished with the rest and they are gone."

The withered old one nodded and proceeded to light his pipe.

"The kow-kow in the kitchen was good," Iliiopoi resumed, licking his lips. "The poi was one-finger, the pig fat, the salmon-belly unstinking, the fish of great freshness and plenty, though the opihis" (tiny, rock-clinging shell-fish) "had been salted and thereby made tough. Never should the opihis be salted. Often have I told you, Kanaka Oolea, that opihis should never be salted. I am full of good kow-kow. My belly is heavy with it. Yet is my heart not light of it because there is no kow-kow in my own house, where is my wife, who is the aunt of your fourth son's second wife, and where is my baby daughter, and my wife's old mother, and my wife's old mother's feeding child that is a cripple, and my wife's sister who lives likewise with us along with her three children, the father being dead of a wicked dropsy--"

"Will five dollars save all of you from funerals for a day or several?" Pool testily cut the tale short.

"Yes, Kanaka Oolea, and as well it will buy my wife a new comb and some tobacco for myself."

From a gold-sack drawn from the hip-pocket of his dungarees, Hardman Pool drew the gold piece and tossed it accurately into the waiting hand.

To a bachelor who wanted six dollars for new leggings, tobacco, and spurs, three dollars were given; the same to another who needed a hat; and to a third, who modestly asked for two dollars, four were given with a flowery-worded compliment anent his prowess in roping a recent wild bull from the mountains. They knew, as a rule, that he cut their requisitions in half, therefore they doubled the size of their requisitions. And Hardman Pool knew they doubled, and smiled to himself. It was his way, and, further, it was a very good way with his multitudinous relatives, and did not reduce his stature in their esteem.

"And you, Ahuhu?" he demanded of one whose name meant "poison- wood."

"And the price of a pair of dungarees," Ahuhu concluded his list of needs. "I have ridden much and hard after your cattle, Kanaka Oolea, and where my dungarees have pressed against the seat of the saddle there is no seat to my dungarees. It is not well that it be said that a Kanaka Oolea cowboy, who is also a cousin of Kanaka Oolea's wife's half-sister, should be shamed to be seen out of the saddle save that he walks backward from all that behold him."

"The price of a dozen pairs of dungarees be thine, Ahuhu," Hardman Pool beamed, tossing to him the necessary sum. "I am proud that my family shares my pride. Afterward, Ahuhu, out of the dozen dungarees you will give me one, else shall I be compelled to walk backward, my own and only dungarees being in like manner well worn and shameful."

And in laughter of love at their haole chief's final sally, all the sweet-child-minded and physically gorgeous company of them departed to their waiting horses, save the old withered one, Kumuhana, who had been bidden to wait.

For a full five minutes they sat in silence. Then Hardman Pool ordered the little maid to fetch a tumbler of gin and milk, which, when she brought it, he nodded her to hand to Kumuhana. The glass did not leave his lips until it was empty, whereon he gave a great audible out-breath of "A-a-ah," and smacked his lips.

"Much awa have I drunk in my time," he said reflectively. "Yet is the awa but a common man's drink, while the haole liquor is a drink for chiefs. The awa has not the liquor's hot willingness, its spur in the ribs of feeling, its biting alive of oneself that is very pleasant since it is pleasant to be alive."

Hardman Pool smiled, nodded agreement, and old Kumuhana continued.

"There is a warmingness to it. It warms the belly and the soul. It warms the heart. Even the soul and the heart grow cold when one is old."

"You ARE old," Pool conceded. "Almost as old as I."

Kumuhana shook his head and murmured. "Were I no older than you I would be as young as you."

"I am seventy-one," said Pool.

"I do not know ages that way," was the reply. "What happened when you were born?"

"Let me see," Pool calculated. "This is 1880. Subtract seventy- one, and it leaves nine. I was born in 1809, which is the year Keliimakai died, which is the year the Scotchman, Archibald Campbell, lived in Honolulu."

"Then am I truly older than you, Kanaka Oolea. I remember the Scotchman well, for I was playing among the grass houses of Honolulu at the time, and already riding a surf-board in the wahine" (woman) "surf at Waikiki. I can take you now to the spot where was the Scotchman's grass house. The Seaman's Mission stands now on the very ground. Yet do I know when I was born. Often my grandmother and my mother told me of it. I was born when Madame

Pele" (the Fire Goddess or Volcano Goddess) "became angry with the people of Paiea because they sacrificed no fish to her from their fish-pool, and she sent down a flow of lava from Huulalai and filled up their pond. For ever was the fish-pond of Paiea filled up. That was when I was born."

"That was in 1801, when James Boyd was building ships for Kamehameha at Hilo," Pool cast back through the calendar; "which makes you seventy-nine, or eight years older than I. You are very old."

"Yes, Kanaka Oolea," muttered Kumuhana, pathetically attempting to swell his shrunken chest with pride.

"And you are very wise."

"Yes, Kanaka Oolea."

"And you know many of the secret things that are known only to old men."

"Yes, Kanaka Oolea."

"And then you know--" Hardman Pool broke off, the more effectively to impress and hypnotize the other ancient with the set stare of his pale-washed blue eyes. "They say the bones of Kahekili were taken from their hiding-place and lie to-day in the Royal Mausoleum. I have heard it whispered that you alone of all living men truly know."

"I know," was the proud answer. "I alone know."

"Well, do they lie there? Yes or no?"

"Kahekili was an alii" (high chief). "It is from this straight line that your wife Kalama came. She is an alii." The old retainer paused and pursed his lean lips in meditation. "I belong to her, as all my people before me belonged to her people before her. She only can command the great secrets of me. She is wise, too wise ever to command me to speak this secret. To you, O Kanaka Oolea, I do not answer yes, I do not answer no. This is a secret of the aliis that even the aliis do not know."

"Very good, Kumuhana," Hardman Pool commanded. "Yet do you forget that I am an alii, and that what my good Kalama does not dare ask, I command to ask. I can send for her, now, and tell her to command your answer. But such would be a foolishness unless you prove yourself doubly foolish. Tell me the secret, and she will never know. A woman's lips must pour out whatever flows in through her ears, being so made. I am a man, and man is differently made. As you well know, my lips suck tight on secrets as a squid sucks to the salty rock. If you will not tell me alone, then will you tell Kalama and me together, and her lips will talk, her lips will talk, so that the latest malahini will shortly know what, otherwise, you and I alone will know."

Long time Kumuhana sat on in silence, debating the argument and finding no way to evade the fact-logic of it.

"Great is your haole wisdom," he conceded at last.

"Yes? or no?" Hardman Pool drove home the point of his steel.

Kumuhana looked about him first, then slowly let his eyes come to rest on the fly-flapping maid.

"Go," Pool commanded her. "And come not back without you hear a clapping of my hands."

Hardman Pool spoke no further, even after the flapper had disappeared into the house; yet his face adamantly looked: "Yes or no?"

Again Kumuhana looked carefully about him, and up into the monkey-pod boughs as if to apprehend a lurking listener. His lips were very dry. With his tongue he moistened them repeatedly. Twice he essayed to speak, but was inarticulately husky. And finally, with bowed head, he whispered, so low and solemnly that Hardman Pool bent his own head to hear: "No."

Pool clapped his hands, and the little maid ran out of the house to him in tremulous, fluttery haste.

"Bring a milk and gin for old Kumuhana, here," Pool commanded; and, to Kumuhana: "Now tell me the whole story."

"Wait," was the answer. "Wait till the little wahine has come and gone."

And when the maid was gone, and the gin and milk had travelled the way predestined of gin and milk when mixed together, Hardman Pool waited without further urge for the story. Kumuhana pressed his hand to his chest and coughed hollowly at intervals, bidding for encouragement; but in the end, of himself, spoke out.

"It was a terrible thing in the old days when a great alii died. Kahekili was a great alii. He might have been king had he lived. Who can tell? I was a young man, not yet married. You know, Kanaka Oolea, when Kahekili died, and you can tell me how old I was. He died when Governor Boki ran the Blonde Hotel here in Honolulu. You have heard?"

"I was still on windward Hawaii," Pool answered. "But I have heard. Boki made a distillery, and leased Manoa lands to grow sugar for it, and Kaahumanu, who was regent, cancelled the lease, rooted out the cane, and planted potatoes. And Boki was angry, and prepared to make war, and gathered his fighting men, with a dozen whaleship deserters and five brass six-pounders, out at Waikiki--"

"That was the very time Kahekili died," Kumuhana broke in eagerly. "You are very wise. You know many things of the old days better than we old kanakas."

"It was 1829," Pool continued complacently. "You were twenty-eight years old, and I was twenty, just coming ashore in the open boat after the burning of the Black Prince."

"I was twenty-eight," Kumuhana resumed. "It sounds right. I remember well Boki's brass guns at Waikiki. Kahekili died, too, at the time, at Waikiki. The people to this day believe his bones were taken to the Hale o Keawe" (mausoleum) "at Honaunau, in Kona-- "

"And long afterward were brought to the Royal Mausoleum here in Honolulu," Pool supplemented.

"Also, Kanaka Oolea, there are some who believe to this day that Queen Alice has them stored with the rest of her ancestral bones in the big jars in her taboo room. All are wrong. I know. The sacred bones of Kahekili are gone and for ever gone. They rest nowhere. They have ceased to be. And many kona winds have whitened the surf at Waikiki since the last man looked upon the last of Kahekili. I alone remain alive of those men. I am the last man, and I was not glad to be at the finish.

"For see! I was a young man, and my heart was white-hot lava for Malia, who was in Kahekili's household. So was Anapuni's heart white-hot for her, though the colour of his heart was black, as you shall see. We were at a drinking that night--Anapuni and I--the night that Kahekili died. Anapuni and I were only commoners, as were all of us kanakas and wahines who were at the drinking with the common sailors and whaleship men from before the mast. We were drinking on the mats by the beach at Waikiki, close to the old heiau" (temple) "that is not far from what is now the Wilders' beach place. I learned then and for ever what quantities of drink haole sailormen can stand. As for us kanakas, our heads were hot and light and rattly as dry gourds with the whisky and the rum.

"It was past midnight, I remember well, when I saw Malia, whom never had I seen at a drinking, come across the wet-hard sand of the beach. My brain burned like red cinders of hell as I looked upon Anapuni look upon her, he being nearest to her by being across from me in the drinking circle. Oh, I know it was whisky and rum and youth that made the heat of me; but there, in that moment, the mad mind of me resolved, if she spoke to him and yielded to dance with him first, that I would put both my hands around his throat and throw him down and under the wahine surf there beside us, and drown and choke out his life and the obstacle of him that stood between me and her. For know, that she had never decided between us, and it was because of him that she was not already and long since mine.

"She was a grand young woman with a body generous as that of a chiefess and more wonderful, as she came upon us, across the wet sand, in the shimmer of the moonlight. Even the haole sailormen made pause of silence, and with open mouths stared upon her. Her walk! I have heard you talk, O Kanaka Oolea, of the woman Helen who caused the war of Troy. I say of Malia that more men would have stormed the walls of hell for her than went against that old-time city of which it is your custom to talk over much and long when you have drunk too little milk and too much gin.

"Her walk! In the moonlight there, the soft glow-fire of the jelly-fishes in the surf like the kerosene-lamp footlights I have seen in the new haole theatre! It was not the walk of a girl, but a woman. She did not flutter forward like rippling wavelets on a reef-sheltered, placid beach. There was that in her manner of walk that was big and queenlike, like the motion of the forces of nature, like the rhythmic flow of lava down the slopes of Kau to the sea, like the movement of the huge orderly trade-wind seas, like the rise and fall of the four great tides of the year that may be like music in the eternal ear of God, being too slow of occurrence in time to make a tune for ordinary quick-pulsing, brief-living, swift-dying man.

"Anapuni was nearest. But she looked at me. Have you ever heard a call, Kanaka Oolea, that is without sound yet is louder than the conches of God? So called she to me across that circle of the drinking. I half arose, for I was not yet full drunken; but Anapuni's arm caught her and drew her, and I sank back on my elbow and watched and raged. He was for making her sit beside him, and I waited. Did she sit, and, next, dance with him, I knew that ere morning Anapuni would be a dead man, choked and drowned by me in the shallow surf.

"Strange, is it not, Kanaka Oolea, all this heat called 'love'? Yet it is not strange. It must be so in the time of one's youth, else would mankind not go on."

"That is why the desire of woman must be greater than the desire of life," Pool concurred. "Else would there be neither men nor women."

"Yes," said Kumuhana. "But it is many a year now since the last of such heat has gone out of me. I remember it as one remembers an old sunrise--a thing that was. And so one grows old, and cold, and drinks gin, not for madness, but for warmth. And the milk is very nourishing.

"But Malia did not sit beside him. I remember her eyes were wild, her hair down and flying, as she bent over him and whispered in his ear. And her hair covered him about and hid him as she whispered, and the sight of it pounded my heart against my ribs and dizzied my head till scarcely could I half-see. And I willed myself with all the will of me that if, in short minutes, she did not come over to me, I would go across the circle and get her.

"It was one of the things never to be. You remember Chief Konukalani? Himself he strode up to the circle. His face was black with anger. He gripped Malia, not by the arm, but by the hair, and dragged her away behind him and was gone. Of that, even now, can I understand not the half. I, who was for slaying Anapuni because of her, raised neither hand nor voice of protest when Konukalani dragged her away by the hair--nor did Anapuni. Of course, we were common men, and he was a chief. That I know. But why should two common men, mad with desire of woman, with desire of woman stronger in them than desire of life, let any one chief, even the highest in the land, drag the woman away by the hair? Desiring her more than life, why should the two men fear to slay then and immediately the one chief? Here is something stronger than life, stronger than woman, but what is it? and why?"

"I will answer you," said Hardman Pool. "It is so because most men are fools, and therefore must be taken care of by the few men who are wise. Such is the secret of chiefship. In all the world are chiefs over men. In all the world that has been have there ever been chiefs, who must say to the many fool men: 'Do this; do not do that. Work, and work as we tell you or your bellies will remain empty and you will perish. Obey the laws we set you or you will be beasts and without place in the world. You would not have been, save for the chiefs before you who ordered and regulated for your fathers. No seed of you will come after you, except that we order and regulate for you now. You must be peace-abiding, and decent, and blow your noses. You must be early to bed of nights, and up early in the morning to work if you would heave beds to sleep in and not roost in trees like the silly fowls. This is the season for the yam-planting and you must plant now. We say now, to-day, and not picnicking and hulaing to-day and yam-planting to-morrow or some other day of the many careless days. You must not kill one another, and you must leave your neighbours' wives alone. All this is life for you, because you think but one day at a time, while we, your chiefs, think for you all days and for days ahead.'"

"Like a cloud on the mountain-top that comes down and wraps about you and that you dimly see is a cloud, so is your wisdom to me, Kanaka Oolea," Kumuhana murmured. "Yet is it sad that I should be born a common man and live all my days a common man."

"That is because you were of yourself common," Hardman Pool assured him. "When a man is born common, and is by nature uncommon, he rises up and overthrows the chiefs and makes himself chief over the chiefs. Why do you not run my ranch, with its many thousands of cattle, and shift the pastures by the rain-fall, and pick the bulls, and arrange the bargaining and the selling of the meat to the sailing ships and war vessels and the people who live in the Honolulu houses, and fight with lawyers, and help make laws, and even tell the King what is wise for him to do and what is dangerous? Why does not any man do this that I do? Any man of all the men who work for me, feed out of my hand, and let me do their thinking for them--me, who work harder than any of them, who eats no more than any of them, and who can sleep on no more than one lauhala mat at a time like any of them?"

"I am out of the cloud, Kanaka Oolea," said Kumuhana, with a visible brightening of countenance. "More clearly do I see. All my long years have the aliis I was born under thought for me. Ever, when I was hungry, I came to them for food, as I come to your kitchen now. Many people eat in your kitchen, and the days of feasts when you slay fat steers for all of us are understandable. It is why I come to you this day, an old man whose labour of strength is not worth a shilling a week, and ask of you twelve dollars to buy a jackass and a second-hand saddle and bridle. It is why twice ten fool men of us, under these monkey-pods half an hour ago, asked of you a dollar or two, or four or five, or ten or twelve. We are the careless ones of the careless days who will not plant the yam in season if our alii does not compel us, who will not think one day for ourselves, and who, when we age to worthlessness, know that our alii will think kow-kow into our bellies and a grass thatch over our heads.

Hardman Pool bowed his appreciation, and urged:

"But the bones of Kahekili. The Chief Konukalani had just dragged away Malia by the hair of the head, and you and Anapuni sat on without protest in the circle of drinking. What was it Malia whispered in Anapuni's ear, bending over him, her hair hiding the face of him?"

"That Kahekili was dead. That was what she whispered to Anapuni. That Kahekili was dead, just dead, and that the chiefs, ordering all within the house to remain within, were debating the disposal of the bones and meat of him before word of his death should get abroad. That the high priest Eoppo was deciding them, and that she had overheard no less than Anapuni and me chosen as the sacrifices to go the way of Kahekili and his bones and to care for him afterward and for ever in the shadowy other world."

"The moepuu, the human sacrifice," Pool commented. "Yet it was nine years since the coming of the missionaries."

"And it was the year before their coming that the idols were cast down and the taboos broken," Kumuhana added. "But the chiefs still practised the old ways, the custom of hunakele, and hid the bones of the aliis where no men should find them and make fish-hooks of their jaws or arrow heads of their long bones for the slaying of little mice in sport. Behold, O Kanaka Oolea!"

The old man thrust out his tongue; and, to Pool's amazement, he saw the surface of that sensitive organ, from root to tip, tattooed in intricate designs.

"That was done after the missionaries came, several years afterward, when Keopuolani died. Also, did I knock out four of my front teeth, and half-circles did I burn over my body with blazing bark. And whoever ventured out-of-doors that night was slain by the chiefs. Nor could a light be shown in a house or a whisper of noise be made. Even dogs and hogs that made a noise were slain, nor all that night were the ships' bells of the haoles in the harbour allowed to strike. It was a terrible thing in those days when an alii died.

"But the night that Kahekili died. We sat on in the drinking circle after Konukalani dragged Malia away by the hair. Some of the haole sailors grumbled; but they were few in the land in those days and the kanakas many. And never was Malia seen of men again. Konukalani alone knew the manner of her slaying, and he never told. And in after years what common men like Anapuni and me should dare to question him?

"Now she had told Anapuni before she was dragged away. But Anapuni's heart was black. Me he did not tell. Worthy he was of the killing I had intended for him. There was a giant harpooner in the circle, whose singing was like the bellowing of bulls; and, gazing on him in amazement while he roared some song of the sea, when next I looked across the circle to Anapuni, Anapuni was gone. He had fled to the high mountains where he could hide with the bird-catchers a week of moons. This I learned afterward.

"I? I sat on, ashamed of my desire of woman that had not been so strong as my slave-obedience to a chief. And I drowned my shame in large drinks of rum and whisky, till the world went round and round, inside my head and out, and the Southern Cross danced a hula in the sky, and the Koolau Mountains bowed their lofty summits to Waikiki and the surf of Waikiki kissed them on their brows. And the giant harpooner was still roaring, his the last sounds in my ear, as I fell back on the lauhala mat, and was to all things for the time as one dead.

"When I awoke was at the faint first beginning of dawn. I was being kicked by a hard naked heel in the ribs. What of the enormousness of the drink I had consumed, the feelings aroused in me by the heel were not pleasant. The kanakas and wahines of the drinking were gone. I alone remained among the sleeping sailormen, the giant harpooner snoring like a whale, his head upon my feet.

"More heel-kicks, and I sat up and was sick. But the one who kicked was impatient, and demanded to know where was Anapuni. And I did not know, and was kicked, this time from both sides by two impatient men, because I did not know. Nor did I know that Kahekili was dead. Yet did I guess something serious was afoot, for the two men who kicked me were chiefs, and no common men crouched behind them to do their bidding. One was Aimoku, of Kaneche; the other Humuhumu, of Manoa.

"They commanded me to go with them, and they were not kind in their commanding; and as I uprose, the head of the giant harpooner was rolled off my feet, past the edge of the mat, into the sand. He grunted like a pig, his lips opened, and all of his tongue rolled out of his mouth into the sand. Nor did he draw it back. For the first time I knew how long was a man's tongue. The sight of the sand on it made me sick for the second time. It is a terrible thing, the next day after a night of drinking. I was afire, dry afire, all the inside of me like a burnt cinder, like aa lava, like the harpooner's tongue dry and gritty with sand. I bent for a half-drunk drinking coconut, but Aimoku kicked it out of my shaking fingers, and Humuhumu smote me with the heel of his hand on my neck.

"They walked before me, side by side, their faces solemn and black, and I walked at their heels. My mouth stank of the drink, and my head was sick with the stale fumes of it, and I would have cut off my right hand for a drink of water, one drink, a mouthful even. And, had I had it, I know it would have sizzled in my belly like water spilled on heated stones for the roasting. It is terrible, the next day after the drinking. All the life-time of many men who died young has passed by me since the last I was able to do such mad drinking of youth when youth knows not capacity and is undeterred.

"But as we went on, I began to know that some alii was dead. No kanakas lay asleep in the sand, nor stole home from their love-making; and no canoes were abroad after the early fish most catchable then inside the reef at the change of the tide. When we came, past the hoiau" (temple), "to where the Great Kamehameha used to haul out his brigs and schooners, I saw, under the canoe-sheds, that the mat-thatches of Kahekili's great double canoe had been taken off, and that even then, at low tide, many men were launching it down across the sand into the water. But all these men were chiefs. And, though my eyes swam, and the inside of my head went around and around, and the inside of my body was a cinder athirst, I guessed that the alii who was dead was Kahekili. For he was old, and most likely of the aliis to be dead."

"It was his death, as I have heard it, more than the intercession of Kekuanaoa, that spoiled Governor Boki's rebellion," Hardman Pool observed.

"It was Kahekili's death that spoiled it," Kumuhana confirmed. "All commoners, when the word slipped out that night of his death, fled into the shelter of the grass houses, nor lighted fire nor pipes, nor breathed loudly, being therein and thereby taboo from use for sacrifice. And all Governor Boki's commoners of fighting men, as well as the haole deserters from ships, so fled, so that the brass guns lay unserved and his handful of chiefs of themselves could do nothing.

"Aimoku and Humuhumu made me sit on the sand to the side from the launching of the great double-canoe. And when it was afloat all the chiefs were athirst, not being used to such toil; and I was told to climb the palms beside the canoe-sheds and throw down drink-coconuts. They drank and were refreshed, but me they refused to let drink.

"Then they bore Kahekili from his house to the canoe in a haole coffin, oiled and varnished and new. It had been made by a ship's carpenter, who thought he was making a boat that must not leak. It was very tight, and over where the face of Kahekili lay was nothing but thin glass. The chiefs had not screwed on the outside plank to cover the glass. Maybe they did not know the manner of haole coffins; but at any rate I was to be glad they did not know, as you shall see.

"'There is but one moepuu,' said the priest Eoppo, looking at me where I sat on the coffin in the bottom of the canoe. Already the chiefs were paddling out through the reef.

"'The other has run into hiding,' Aimoku answered. 'This one was all we could get.'

"And then I knew. I knew everything. I was to be sacrificed. Anapuni had been planned for the other sacrifice. That was what Malia had whispered to Anapuni at the drinking. And she had been dragged away before she could tell me. And in his blackness of heart he had not told me.

"'There should be two,' said Eoppo. 'It is the law.'

"Aimoku stopped paddling and looked back shoreward as if to return and get a second sacrifice. But several of the chiefs contended no, saying that all commoners were fled to the mountains or were lying taboo in their houses, and that it might take days before they could catch one. In the end Eoppo gave in, though he grumbled from time to time that the law required two moepuus.

"We paddled on, past Diamond Head and abreast of Koko Head, till we were in the midway of the Molokai Channel. There was quite a sea running, though the trade wind was blowing light. The chiefs rested from their paddles, save for the steersmen who kept the canoes bow-on to the wind and swell. And, ere they proceeded further in the matter, they opened more coconuts and drank.

"'I do not mind so much being the moepuu,' I said to Humuhumu; 'but I should like to have a drink before I am slain.' I got no drink. But I spoke true. I was too sick of the much whisky and rum to be afraid to die. At least my mouth would stink no more, nor my head ache, nor the inside of me be as dry-hot sand. Almost worst of all, I suffered at thought of the harpooner's tongue, as last I had seen it lying on the sand and covered with sand. O Kanaka Oolea, what animals young men are with the drink! Not until they have grown old, like you and me, do they control their wantonness of thirst and drink sparingly, like you and me."

"Because we have to," Hardman Pool rejoined. "Old stomachs are worn thin and tender, and we drink sparingly because we dare not drink more. We are wise, but the wisdom is bitter."

"The priest Eoppo sang a long mele about Kahekili's mother and his mother's mother, and all their mothers all the way back to the beginning of time," Kumuhana resumed. "And it seemed I must die of my sand-hot dryness ere he was done. And he called upon all the gods of the under world, the middle world and the over world, to care for and cherish the dead alii about to be consigned to them, and to carry out the curses--they were terrible curses--he laid upon all living men and men to live after who might tamper with the bones of Kahekili to use them in sport of vermin-slaying.

"Do you know, Kanaka Oolea, the priest talked a language largely different, and I know it was the priest language, the old language. Maui he did not name Maui, but Maui-Tiki-Tiki and Maui-Po-Tiki. And Hina, the goddess-mother of Maui, he named Ina. And Maui's god-father he named sometimes Akalana and sometimes Kanaloa. Strange how one about to die and very thirsty should remember such things! And I remember the priest named Hawaii as Vaii, and Lanai as Ngangai."

"Those were the Maori names," Hardman Pool explained, "and the Samoan and Tongan names, that the priests brought with them in their first voyages from the south in the long ago when they found Hawaii and settled to dwell upon it."

"Great is your wisdom, O Kanaka Oolea," the old man accorded solemnly. "Ku, our Supporter of the Heavens, the priest named Tu, and also Ru; and La, our God of the Sun, he named Ra--"

"And Ra was a sun-god in Egypt in the long ago," Pool interrupted with a sparkle of interest. "Truly, you Polynesians have travelled far in time and space since first you began. A far cry it is from Old Egypt, when Atlantis was still afloat, to Young Hawaii in the North Pacific. But proceed, Kumuhana. Do you remember anything also of what the priest Eoppo sang?"

"At the very end," came the confirming nod, "though I was near dead myself, and nearer to die under the priest's knife, he sang what I have remembered every word of. Listen! It was thus."

And in quavering falsetto, with the customary broken-notes, the old man sang.

"A Maori death-chant unmistakable," Pool exclaimed, "sung by an Hawaiian with a tattooed tongue! Repeat it once again, and I shall say it to you in English."

And when it had been repeated, he spoke it slowly in English:

"But death is nothing new. Death is and has been ever since old Maui died. Then Pata-tai laughed loud And woke the goblin-god, Who severed him in two, and shut him in, So dusk of eve came on."

"And at the last," Kumuhana resumed, "I was not slain. Eoppo, the killing knife in hand and ready to lift for the blow, did not lift. And I? How did I feel and think? Often, Kanaka Oolea, have I since laughed at the memory of it. I felt very thirsty. I did not want to die. I wanted a drink of water. I knew I was going to die, and I kept remembering the thousand waterfalls falling to waste down the pans" (precipices) "of the windward Koolau Mountains. I did not think of Anapuni. I was too thirsty. I did not think of Malia. I was too thirsty. But continually, inside my head, I saw the tongue of the harpooner, covered dry with sand, as I had last seen it, lying in the sand. My tongue was like that, too. And in the bottom of the canoe rolled about many drinking nuts. Yet I did not attempt to drink, for these were chiefs and I was a common man.

"'No,' said Eoppo, commanding the chiefs to throw overboard the coffin. 'There are not two moepuus, therefore there shall be none.'

"'Slay the one,' the chiefs cried.

"But Eoppo shook his head, and said: 'We cannot send Kahekili on his way with only the tops of the taro.'

"'Half a fish is better than none,' Aimoku said the old saying.

"'Not at the burying of an alii,' was the priest's quick reply. 'It is the law. We cannot be niggard with Kahekili and cut his allotment of sacrifice in half.'

"So, for the moment, while the coffin went overside, I was not slain. And it was strange that I was glad immediately that I was to live. And I began to remember Malia, and to begin to plot a vengeance on Anapuni. And with the blood of life thus freshening in me, my thirst multiplied on itself tenfold and my tongue and mouth and throat seemed as sanded as the tongue of the harpooner. The coffin being overboard, I was sitting in the bottom of the canoe. A coconut rolled between my legs and I closed them on it. But as I picked it up in my hand, Aimoku smote my hand with the paddle-edge. Behold!"

He held up the hand, showing two fingers crooked from never having been set.

"I had no time to vex over my pain, for worse things were upon me. All the chiefs were crying out in horror. The coffin, head-end up, had not sunk. It bobbed up and down in the sea astern of us. And the canoe, without way on it, bow-on to sea and wind, was drifted down by sea and wind upon the coffin. And the glass of it was to us, so that we could see the face and head of Kahekili through the glass; and he grinned at us through the glass and seemed alive already in the other world and angry with us, and, with other-world power, about to wreak his anger upon us. Up and down he bobbed, and the canoe drifted closer upon him.

"'Kill him!' 'Bleed him!' 'Thrust to the heart of him!' These things the chiefs were crying out to Eoppo in their fear. 'Over with the taro tops!' 'Let the alii have the half of a fish!'

"Eoppo, priest though he was, was likewise afraid, and his reason weakened before the sight of Kahekili in his haole coffin that would not sink. He seized me by the hair, drew me to my feet, and lifted the knife to plunge to my heart. And there was no resistance in me. I knew again only that I was very thirsty, and before my swimming eyes, in mid-air and close up, dangled the sanded tongue of the harpooner.

"But before the knife could fall and drive in, the thing happened that saved me. Akai, half-brother to Governor Boki, as you will remember, was steersman of the canoe, and, therefore, in the stern, was nearest to the coffin and its dead that would not sink. He was wild with fear, and he thrust out with the point of his paddle to fend off the coffined alii that seemed bent to come on board. The point of the paddle struck the glass. The glass broke--"

"And the coffin immediately sank," Hardman Pool broke in; "the air that floated it escaping through the broken glass."

"The coffin immediately sank, being built by the ship's carpenter like a boat," Kumuhana confirmed. "And I, who was a moepuu, became a man once more. And I lived, though I died a thousand deaths from thirst before we gained back to the beach at Waikiki.

"And so, O Kanaka Oolea, the bones of Kahekili do not lie in the Royal Mausoleum. They are at the bottom of Molokai Channel, if not, long since, they have become floating dust of slime, or, built into the bodies of the coral creatures dead and gone, are built into the coral reef itself. Of men I am the one living who saw the bones of Kahekili sink into the Molokai Channel."

In the pause that followed, wherein Hardman Pool was deep sunk in meditation, Kumuhana licked his dry lips many times. At the last he broke silence:

"The twelve dollars, Kanaka Oolea, for the jackass and the second- hand saddle and bridle?"

"The twelve dollars would be thine," Pool responded, passing to the ancient one six dollars and a half, "save that I have in my stable junk the very bridle and saddle for you which I shall give you. These six dollars and a half will buy you the perfectly suitable jackass of the pake" (Chinese) "at Kokako who told me only yesterday that such was the price."

They sat on, Pool meditating, conning over and over to himself the Maori death-chant he had heard, and especially the line, "So dusk of eve came on," finding in it an intense satisfaction of beauty; Kumuhana licking his lips and tokening that he waited for something more. At last he broke silence.

"I have talked long, O Kanaka Oolea. There is not the enduring moistness in my mouth that was when I was young. It seems that afresh upon me is the thirst that was mine when tormented by the visioned tongue of the harpooner. The gin and milk is very good, O Kanaka Oolea, for a tongue that is like the harpooner's."

A shadow of a smile flickered across Pool's face. He clapped his hands, and the little maid came running.

"Bring one glass of gin and milk for old Kumuhana," commanded Hardman Pool.
WAIKIKI, HONOLULU June 28, 1916.

When Alice Told her Soul

This, of Alice Akana, is an affair of Hawaii, not of this day, but of days recent enough, when Abel Ah Yo preached his famous revival in Honolulu and persuaded Alice Akana to tell her soul. But what Alice told concerned itself with the earlier history of the then surviving generation.

For Alice Akana was fifty years old, had begun life early, and, early and late, lived it spaciously. What she knew went back into the roots and foundations of families, businesses, and plantations. She was the one living repository of accurate information that lawyers sought out, whether the information they required related to land-boundaries and land gifts, or to marriages, births, bequests, or scandals. Rarely, because of the tight tongue she kept behind her teeth, did she give them what they asked; and when she did was when only equity was served and no one was hurt.

For Alice had lived, from early in her girlhood, a life of flowers, and song, and wine, and dance; and, in her later years, had herself been mistress of these revels by office of mistress of the hula house. In such atmosphere, where mandates of God and man and caution are inhibited, and where woozled tongues will wag, she acquired her historical knowledge of things never otherwise whispered and rarely guessed. And her tight tongue had served her well, so that, while the old-timers knew she must know, none ever heard her gossip of the times of Kalakaua's boathouse, nor of the high times of officers of visiting warships, nor of the diplomats and ministers and councils of the countries of the world.

So, at fifty, loaded with historical dynamite sufficient, if it were ever exploded, to shake the social and commercial life of the Islands, still tight of tongue, Alice Akana was mistress of the hula house, manageress of the dancing girls who hula'd for royalty, for luaus (feasts), house-parties, poi suppers, and curious tourists. And, at fifty, she was not merely buxom, but short and fat in the Polynesian peasant way, with a constitution and lack of organic weakness that promised incalculable years. But it was at fifty that she strayed, quite by chance of time and curiosity, into Abel Ah Yo's revival meeting.

Now Abel Ah Yo, in his theology and word wizardry, was as much mixed a personage as Billy Sunday. In his genealogy he was much more mixed, for he was compounded of one-fourth Portuguese, one- fourth Scotch, one-fourth Hawaiian, and one-fourth Chinese. The Pentecostal fire he flamed forth was hotter and more variegated than could any one of the four races of him alone have flamed forth. For in him were gathered together the cannyness and the cunning, the wit and the wisdom, the subtlety and the rawness, the passion and the philosophy, the agonizing spirit-groping and he legs up to the knees in the dung of reality, of the four radically different breeds that contributed to the sum of him. His, also, was the clever self-deceivement of the entire clever compound.

When it came to word wizardry, he had Billy Sunday, master of slang and argot of one language, skinned by miles. For in Abel Ah Yo were the five verbs, and nouns, and adjectives, and metaphors of four living languages. Intermixed and living promiscuously and vitally together, he possessed in these languages a reservoir of expression in which a myriad Billy Sundays could drown. Of no race, a mongrel par excellence, a heterogeneous scrabble, the genius of the admixture was superlatively Abel Ah Yo's. Like a chameleon, he titubated and scintillated grandly between the diverse parts of him, stunning by frontal attack and surprising and confouding by flanking sweeps the mental homogeneity of the more simply constituted souls who came in to his revival to sit under him and flame to his flaming.

Abel Ah Yo believed in himself and his mixedness, as he believed in the mixedness of his weird concept that God looked as much like him as like any man, being no mere tribal god, but a world god that must look equally like all races of all the world, even if it led to piebaldness. And the concept worked. Chinese, Korean, Japanese, Hawaiian, Porto Rican, Russian, English, French--members of all races--knelt without friction, side by side, to his revision of deity.

Himself in his tender youth an apostate to the Church of England, Abel Ah Yo had for years suffered the lively sense of being a Judas sinner. Essentially religious, he had foresworn the Lord. Like Judas therefore he was. Judas was damned. Wherefore he, Abel Ah Yo, was damned; and he did not want to be damned. So, quite after the manner of humans, he squirmed and twisted to escape damnation. The day came when he solved his escape. The doctrine that Judas was damned, he concluded, was a misinterpretation of God, who, above all things, stood for justice. Judas had been God's servant, specially selected to perform a particularly nasty job. Therefore Judas, ever faithful, a betrayer only by divine command, was a saint. Ergo, he, Abel Ah Yo, was a saint by very virtue of his apostasy to a particular sect, and he could have access with clear grace any time to God.

This theory became one of the major tenets of his preaching, and was especially efficacious in cleansing the consciences of the back-sliders from all other faiths who else, in the secrecy of their subconscious selves, were being crushed by the weight of the Judas sin. To Abel Ah Yo, God's plan was as clear as if he, Abel Ah Yo, had planned it himself. All would be saved in the end, although some took longer than others, and would win only to backseats. Man's place in the ever-fluxing chaos of the world was definite and pre-ordained--if by no other token, then by denial that there was any ever-fluxing chaos. This was a mere bugbear of mankind's addled fancy; and, by stinging audacities of thought and speech, by vivid slang that bit home by sheerest intimacy into his listeners' mental processes, he drove the bugbear from their brains, showed them the loving clarity of God's design, and, thereby, induced in them spiritual serenity and calm.

What chance had Alice Akana, herself pure and homogeneous Hawaiian, against his subtle, democratic-tinged, four-race-engendered, slang- munitioned attack? He knew, by contact, almost as much as she about the waywardness of living and sinning--having been singing boy on the passenger-ships between Hawaii and California, and, after that, bar boy, afloat and ashore, from the Barbary Coast to Heinie's Tavern. In point of fact, he had left his job of Number One Bar Boy at the University Club to embark on his great preachment revival.

So, when Alice Akana strayed in to scoff, she remained to pray to Abel Ah Yo's god, who struck her hard-headed mind as the most sensible god of which she had ever heard. She gave money into Abel Ah Yo's collection plate, closed up the hula house, and dismissed the hula dancers to more devious ways of earning a livelihood, shed her bright colours and raiments and flower garlands, and bought a Bible.

It was a time of religious excitement in the purlieus of Honolulu. The thing was a democratic movement of the people toward God. Place and caste were invited, but never came. The stupid lowly, and the humble lowly, only, went down on its knees at the penitent form, admitted its pathological weight and hurt of sin, eliminated and purged all its bafflements, and walked forth again upright under the sun, child-like and pure, upborne by Abel Ah Yo's god's arm around it. In short, Abel Ah Yo's revival was a clearing house for sin and sickness of spirit, wherein sinners were relieved of their burdens and made light and bright and spiritually healthy again.

But Alice was not happy. She had not been cleared. She bought and dispersed Bibles, contributed more money to the plate, contralto'd gloriously in all the hymns, but would not tell her soul. In vain Abel Ah Yo wrestled with her. She would not go down on her knees at the penitent form and voice the things of tarnish within her-- the ill things of good friends of the old days. "You cannot serve two masters," Abel Ah Yo told her. "Hell is full of those who have tried. Single of heart and pure of heart must you make your peace with God. Not until you tell your soul to God right out in meeting will you be ready for redemption. In the meantime you will suffer the canker of the sin you carry about within you."

Scientifically, though he did not know it and though he continually jeered at science, Abel Ah Yo was right. Not could she be again as a child and become radiantly clad in God's grace, until she had eliminated from her soul, by telling, all the sophistications that had been hers, including those she shared with others. In the Protestant way, she must bare her soul in public, as in the Catholic way it was done in the privacy of the confessional. The result of such baring would be unity, tranquillity, happiness, cleansing, redemption, and immortal life.

"Choose!" Abel Ah Yo thundered. "Loyalty to God, or loyalty to man." And Alice could not choose. Too long had she kept her tongue locked with the honour of man. "I will tell all my soul about myself," she contended. "God knows I am tired of my soul and should like to have it clean and shining once again as when I was a little girl at Kaneohe--"

"But all the corruption of your soul has been with other souls," was Abel Ah Yo's invariable reply. "When you have a burden, lay it down. You cannot bear a burden and be quit of it at the same time."

"I will pray to God each day, and many times each day," she urged. "I will approach God with humility, with sighs and with tears. I will contribute often to the plate, and I will buy Bibles, Bibles, Bibles without end."

"And God will not smile upon you," God's mouthpiece retorted. "And you will remain weary and heavy-laden. For you will not have told all your sin, and not until you have told all will you be rid of any."

"This rebirth is difficult," Alice sighed.

"Rebirth is even more difficult than birth." Abel Ah Yo did anything but comfort her. "'Not until you become as a little child . . .'"

"If ever I tell my soul, it will be a big telling," she confided.

"The bigger the reason to tell it then."

And so the situation remained at deadlock, Abel Ah Yo demanding absolute allegiance to God, and Alice Akana flirting on the fringes of paradise.

"You bet it will be a big telling, if Alice ever begins," the beach-combing and disreputable kamaainas (old-timers) gleefully told one another over their Palm Tree gin.

In the clubs the possibility of her telling was of more moment. The younger generation of men announced that they had applied for front seats at the telling, while many of the older generation of men joked hollowly about the conversion of Alice. Further, Alice found herself abruptly popular with friends who had forgotten her existence for twenty years.

One afternoon, as Alice, Bible in hand, was taking the electric street car at Hotel and Fort, Cyrus Hodge, sugar factor and magnate, ordered his chauffeur to stop beside her. Willy nilly, in excess of friendliness, he had her into his limousine beside him and went three-quarters of an hour out of his way and time personally to conduct her to her destination.

"Good for sore eyes to see you," he burbled. "How the years fly! You're looking fine. The secret of youth is yours."

Alice smiled and complimented in return in the royal Polynesian way of friendliness.

"My, my," Cyrus Hodge reminisced. "I was such a boy in those days!"

"SOME boy," she laughed acquiescence.

"But knowing no more than the foolishness of a boy in those long- ago days."

"Remember the night your hack-driver got drunk and left you--"

"S-s-sh!" he cautioned. "That Jap driver is a high-school graduate and knows more English than either of us. Also, I think he is a spy for his Government. So why should we tell him anything? Besides, I was so very young. You remember . . . "

"Your cheeks were like the peaches we used to grow before the Mediterranean fruit fly got into them," Alice agreed. "I don't think you shaved more than once a week then. You were a pretty boy. Don't you remember the hula we composed in your honour, the-- "

"S-s-sh!" he hushed her. "All that's buried and forgotten. May it remain forgotten."

And she was aware that in his eyes was no longer any of the ingenuousness of youth she remembered. Instead, his eyes were keen and speculative, searching into her for some assurance that she would not resurrect his particular portion of that buried past.

"Religion is a good thing for us as we get along into middle age," another old friend told her. He was building a magnificent house on Pacific Heights, but had recently married a second time, and was even then on his way to the steamer to welcome home his two daughters just graduated from Vassar. "We need religion in our old age, Alice. It softens, makes us more tolerant and forgiving of the weaknesses of others--especially the weaknesses of youth of--of others, when they played high and low and didn't know what they were doing."

He waited anxiously.

"Yes," she said. "We are all born to sin and it is hard to grow out of sin. But I grow, I grow."

"Don't forget, Alice, in those other days I always played square. You and I never had a falling out."

"Not even the night you gave that luau when you were twenty-one and insisted on breaking the glassware after every toast. But of course you paid for it."

"Handsomely," he asserted almost pleadingly.

"Handsomely," she agreed. "I replaced more than double the quantity with what you paid me, so that at the next luau I catered one hundred and twenty plates without having to rent or borrow a dish or glass. Lord Mainweather gave that luau--you remember him."

"I was pig-sticking with him at Mana," the other nodded. "We were at a two weeks' house-party there. But say, Alice, as you know, I think this religion stuff is all right and better than all right. But don't let it carry you off your feet. And don't get to telling your soul on me. What would my daughters think of that broken glassware!"

"I always did have an aloha" (warm regard) "for you, Alice," a member of the Senate, fat and bald-headed, assured her.

And another, a lawyer and a grandfather: "We were always friends, Alice. And remember, any legal advice or handling of business you may require, I'll do for you gladly, and without fees, for the sake of our old-time friendship."

Came a banker to her late Christmas Eve, with formidable, legal- looking envelopes in his hand which he presented to her.

"Quite by chance," he explained, "when my people were looking up land-records in Iapio Valley, I found a mortgage of two thousand on your holdings there--that rice land leased to Ah Chin. And my mind drifted back to the past when we were all young together, and wild- -a bit wild, to be sure. And my heart warmed with the memory of you, and, so, just as an aloha, here's the whole thing cleared off for you."

Nor was Alice forgotten by her own people. Her house became a Mecca for native men and women, usually performing pilgrimage privily after darkness fell, with presents always in their hands-- squid fresh from the reef, opihis and limu, baskets of alligator pears, roasting corn of the earliest from windward Cahu, mangoes and star-apples, taro pink and royal of the finest selection, sucking pigs, banana poi, breadfruit, and crabs caught the very day from Pearl Harbour. Mary Mendana, wife of the Portuguese Consul, remembered her with a five-dollar box of candy and a mandarin coat that would have fetched three-quarters of a hundred dollars at a fire sale. And Elvira Miyahara Makaena Yin Wap, the wife of Yin Wap the wealthy Chinese importer, brought personally to Alice two entire bolts of pina cloth from the Philippines and a dozen pairs of silk stockings.

The time passed, and Abel Ah Yo struggled with Alice for a properly penitent heart, and Alice struggled with herself for her soul, while half of Honolulu wickedly or apprehensively hung on the outcome. Carnival week was over, polo and the races had come and gone, and the celebration of Fourth of July was ripening, ere Abel Ah Yo beat down by brutal psychology the citadel of her reluctance. It was then that he gave his famous exhortation which might be summed up as Abel Ah Yo's definition of eternity. Of course, like Billy Sunday on certain occasions, Abel Ah Yo had cribbed the definition. But no one in the Islands knew it, and his rating as a revivalist uprose a hundred per cent.

So successful was his preaching that night, that he reconverted many of his converts, who fell and moaned about the penitent form and crowded for room amongst scores of new converts burnt by the pentecostal fire, including half a company of negro soldiers from the garrisoned Twenty-Fifth Infantry, a dozen troopers from the Fourth Cavalry on its way to the Philippines, as many drunken man- of-war's men, divers ladies from Iwilei, and half the riff-raff of the beach.

Abel Ah Yo, subtly sympathetic himself by virtue of his racial admixture, knowing human nature like a book and Alice Akana even more so, knew just what he was doing when he arose that memorable night and exposited God, hell, and eternity in terms of Alice Akana's comprehension. For, quite by chance, he had discovered her cardinal weakness. First of all, like all Polynesians, an ardent lover of nature, he found that earthquake and volcanic eruption were the things of which Alice lived in terror. She had been, in the past, on the Big Island, through cataclysms that had slacken grass houses down upon her while she slept, and she had beheld Madame Pele (the Fire or Volcano Goddess) fling red-fluxing lava down the long slopes of Mauna Loa, destroying fish-ponds on the sea-brim and licking up droves of beef cattle, villages, and humans on her fiery way.

The night before, a slight earthquake had shaken Honolulu and given Alice Akana insomnia. And the morning papers had stated that Mauna Kea had broken into eruption, while the lava was rising rapidly in the great pit of Kilauea. So, at the meeting, her mind vexed between the terrors of this world and the delights of the eternal world to come, Alice sat down in a front seat in a very definite state of the "jumps."

And Abel Ah Yo arose and put his finger on the sorest part of her soul. Sketching the nature of God in the stereotyped way, but making the stereotyped alive again with his gift of tongues in Pidgin-English and Pidgin-Hawaiian, Abel Ah Yo described the day when the Lord, even His infinite patience at an end, would tell Peter to close his day book and ledgers, command Gabriel to summon all souls to Judgment, and cry out with a voice of thunder: "Welakahao!"

This anthromorphic deity of Abel Ah Yo thundering the modern Hawaiian-English slang of welakahao at the end of the world, is a fair sample of the revivalist's speech-tools of discourse.

Welakahao means literally "hot iron." It was coined in the Honolulu Iron-works by the hundreds of Hawaiian men there employed, who meant by it "to hustle," "to get a move on," the iron being hot meaning that the time had come to strike.

"And the Lord cried 'Welakahao,' and the Day of Judgment began and was over wiki-wiki" (quickly) "just like that; for Peter was a better bookkeeper than any on the Waterhouse Trust Company Limited, and, further, Peter's books were true."

Swiftly Abel Ah Yo divided the sheep from the goats, and hastened the latter down into hell.

"And now," he demanded, perforce his language on these pages being properly Englished, "what is hell like? Oh, my friends, let me describe to you, in a little way, what I have beheld with my own eyes on earth of the possibilities of hell. I was a young man, a boy, and I was at Hilo. Morning began with earthquakes. Throughout the day the mighty land continued to shake and tremble, till strong men became seasick, and women clung to trees to escape falling, and cattle were thrown down off their feet. I beheld myself a young calf so thrown. A night of terror indescribable followed. The land was in motion like a canoe in a Kona gale. There was an infant crushed to death by its fond mother stepping upon it whilst fleeing her falling house.

"The heavens were on fire above us. We read our Bibles by the light of the heavens, and the print was fine, even for young eyes. Those missionary Bibles were always too small of print. Forty miles away from us, the heart of hell burst from the lofty mountains and gushed red-blood of fire-melted rock toward the sea. With the heavens in vast conflagration and the earth hulaing beneath our feet, was a scene too awful and too majestic to be enjoyed. We could think only of the thin bubble-skin of earth between us and the everlasting lake of fire and brimstone, and of God to whom we prayed to save us. There were earnest and devout souls who there and then promised their pastors to give not their shaved tithes, but five-tenths of their all to the church, if only the Lord would let them live to contribute.

"Oh, my friends, God saved us. But first he showed us a foretaste of that hell that will yawn for us on the last day, when he cries 'Welakahao!' in a voice of thunder. When the iron is hot! Think of it! When the iron is hot for sinners!

"By the third day, things being much quieter, my friend the preacher and I, being calm in the hand of God, journeyed up Mauna Loa and gazed into the awful pit of Kilauea. We gazed down into the fathomless abyss to the lake of fire far below, roaring and dashing its fiery spray into billows and fountaining hundreds of feet into the air like Fourth of July fireworks you have all seen, and all the while we werc suffocating and made dizzy by the immense volumes of smoke and brimstone ascending.

"And I say unto you, no pious person could gaze down upon that scene without recognizing fully the Bible picture of the Pit of Hell. Believe me, the writers of the New Testament had nothing on us. As for me, my eyes were fixed upon the exhibition before me, and I stood mute and trembling under a sense never before so fully realized of the power, the majesty, and terror of Almighty God--the resources of His wrath, and the untold horrors of the finally impenitent who do not tell their souls and make their peace with the Creator. {1}

"But oh, my friends, think you our guides, our native attendants, deep-sunk in heathenism, were affected by such a scene? No. The devil's hand was upon them. Utterly regardless and unimpressed, they were only careful about their supper, chatted about their raw fish, and stretched themselves upon their mats to sleep. Children of the devil they were, insensible to the beauties, the sublimities, and the awful terror of God's works. But you are not heathen I now address. What is a heathen? He is one who betrays a stupid insensibility to every elevated idea and to every elevated emotion. If you wish to awaken his attention, do not bid him to look down into the Pit of Hell. But present him with a calabash of poi, a raw fish, or invite him to some low, grovelling, and sensuous sport. Oh, my friends, how lost are they to all that elevates the immortal soul! But the preacher and I, sad and sick at heart for them, gazed down into hell. Oh, my friends, it WAS hell, the hell of the Scriptures, the hell of eternal torment for the undeserving . . . "

Alice Akana was in an ecstasy or hysteria of terror. She was mumbling incoherently: "O Lord, I will give nine-tenths of my all. I will give all. I will give even the two bolts of pina cloth, the mandarin coat, and the entire dozen silk stockings . . . "

By the time she could lend ear again, Abel Ah Yo was launching out on his famous definition of eternity.

"Eternity is a long time, my friends. God lives, and, therefore, God lives inside eternity. And God is very old. The fires of hell are as old and as everlasting as God. How else could there be everlasting torment for those sinners cast down by God into the Pit on the Last Day to burn for ever and for ever through all eternity? Oh, my friends, your minds are small--too small to grasp eternity. Yet is it given to me, by God's grace, to convey to you an understanding of a tiny bit of eternity.

"The grains of sand on the beach of Waikiki are as many as the stars, and more. No man may count them. Did he have a million lives in which to count them, he would have to ask for more time. Now let us consider a little, dinky, old minah bird with one broken wing that cannot fly. At Waikiki the minah bird that cannot fly takes one grain of sand in its beak and hops, hops, all day lone and for many days, all the day to Pearl Harbour and drops that one grain of sand into the harbour. Then it hops, hops, all day and for many days, all the way back to Waikiki for another grain of sand. And again it hops, hops all the way back to Pearl Harbour. And it continues to do this through the years and centuries, and the thousands and thousands of centuries, until, at last, there remains not one grain of sand at Waikiki and Pearl Harbour is filled up with land and growing coconuts and pine-apples. And then, oh my friends, even then, IT WOULD NOT YET BE SUNRISE IN HELL!

Here, at the smashing impact of so abrupt a climax, unable to withstand the sheer simplicity and objectivity of such artful measurement of a trifle of eternity, Alice Akana's mind broke down and blew up. She uprose, reeled blindly, and stumbled to her knees at the penitent form. Abel Ah Yo had not finished his preaching, but it was his gift to know crowd psychology, and to feel the heat of the pentecostal conflagration that scorched his audience. He called for a rousing revival hymn from his singers, and stepped down to wade among the hallelujah-shouting negro soldiers to Alice Akana. And, ere the excitement began to ebb, nine-tenths of his congregation and all his converts were down on knees and praying and shouting aloud an immensity of contriteness and sin.

Word came, via telephone, almost simultaneously to the Pacific and University Clubs, that at last Alice was telling her soul in meeting; and, by private machine and taxi-cab, for the first time Abel Ah Yo's revival was invaded by those of caste and place. The first comers beheld the curious sight of Hawaiian, Chinese, and all variegated racial mixtures of the smelting-pot of Hawaii, men and women, fading out and slinking away through the exits of Abel Ah Yo's tabernacle. But those who were sneaking out were mostly men, while those who remained were avid-faced as they hung on Alice's utterance.

Never was a more fearful and damning community narrative enunciated in the entire

Pacific, north and south, than that enunciated by Alice Akana; the penitent Phryne of Honolulu.

"Huh!" the first comers heard her saying, having already disposed of most of the venial sins of the lesser ones of her memory. "You think this man, Stephen Makekau, is the son of Moses Makekau and Minnie Ah Ling, and has a legal right to the two hundred and eight dollars he draws down each month from Parke Richards Limited, for the lease of the fish-pond to Bill Kong at Amana. Not so. Stephen Makekau is not the son of Moses. He is the son of Aaron Kama and Tillie Naone. He was given as a present, as a feeding child, to Moses and Minnie, by Aaron and Tillie. I know. Moses and Minnie and Aaron and Tillie are dead. Yet I know and can prove it. Old Mrs. Poepoe is still alive. I was present when Stephen was born, and in the night-time, when he was two months old, I myself carried him as a present to Moses and Minnie, and old Mrs. Poepoe carried the lantern. This secret has been one of my sins. It has kept me from God. Now I am free of it. Young Archie Makekau, who collects bills for the Gas Company and plays baseball in the afternoons, and drinks too much gin, should get that two hundred and eight dollars the first of each month from Parke Richards Limited. He will blow it in on gin and a Ford automobile. Stephen is a good man. Archie is no good. Also he is a liar, and he has served two sentences on the reef, and was in reform school before that. Yet God demands the truth, and Archie will get the money and make a bad use of it."

And in such fashion Alice rambled on through the experiences of her long and full-packed life. And women forgot they were in the tabernacle, and men too, and faces darkened with passion as they learned for the first time the long-buried secrets of their other halves.

"The lawyers' offices will be crowded to-morrow morning," MacIlwaine, chief of detectives, paused long enough from storing away useful information to lean and mutter in Colonel Stilton's ear.

Colonel Stilton grinned affirmation, although the chief of detectives could not fail to note the ghastliness of the grin.

"There is a banker in Honolulu. You all know his name. He is 'way up, swell society because of his wife. He owns much stock in General Plantations and Inter-Island."

MacIlwaine recognized the growing portrait and forbore to chuckle.

"His name is Colonel Stilton. Last Christmas Eve he came to my house with big aloha" (love) "and gave me mortgages on my land in Iapio Valley, all cancelled, for two thousand dollars' worth. Now why did he have such big cash aloha for me? I will tell you . . . "

And tell she did, throwing the searchlight on ancient business transactions and political deals which from their inception had lurked in the dark.

"This," Alice concluded the episode, "has long been a sin upon my conscience, and kept my heart from God.

"And Harold Miles was that time President of the Senate, and next week he bought three town lots at Pearl Harbour, and painted his Honolulu house, and paid up his back dues in his clubs. Also the Ramsay home at Honokiki was left by will to the people if the Government would keep it up. But if the Government, after two years, did not begin to keep it up, then would it go to the Ramsay heirs, whom old Ramsay hated like poison. Well, it went to the heirs all right. Their lawyer was Charley Middleton, and he had me help fix it with the Government men. And their names were . . . " Six names, from both branches of the Legislature, Alice recited, and added: "Maybe they all painted their houses after that. For the first time have I spoken. My heart is much lighter and softer. It has been coated with an armour of house-paint against the Lord. And there is Harry Werther. He was in the Senate that time. Everybody said bad things about him, and he was never re-elected. Yet his house was not painted. He was honest. To this day his house is not painted, as everybody knows.

"There is Jim Lokendamper. He has a bad heart. I heard him, only last week, right here before you all, tell his soul. He did not tell all his soul, and he lied to God. I am not lying to God. It is a big telling, but I am telling everything. Now Azalea Akau, sitting right over there, is his wife. But Lizzie Lokendamper is his married wife. A long time ago he had the great aloha for Azalea. You think her uncle, who went to California and died, left her by will that two thousand five hundred dollars she got. Her uncle did not. I know. Her uncle cried broke in California, and Jim Lokendamper sent eighty dollars to California to bury him. Jim Lokendamper had a piece of land in Kohala he got from his mother's aunt. Lizzie, his married wife, did not know this. So he sold it to the Kohala Ditch Company and wave the twenty-five hundred to Azalea Akau--"

Here, Lizzie, the married wife, upstood like a fury long-thwarted, and, in lieu of her husband, already fled, flung herself tooth and nail on Azalea.

"Wait, Lizzie Lokendamper!" Alice cried out. "I have much weight of you on my heart and some house-paint too . . . "

And when she had finished her disclosure of how Lizzie had painted her house, Azalea was up and raging.

"Wait, Azalea Akau. I shall now lighten my heart about you. And it is not house-paint. Jim always paid that. It is your new bath-tub and modern plumbing that is heavy on me . . . "

Worse, much worse, about many and sundry, did Alice Akana have to say, cutting high in business, financial, and social life, as well as low. None was too high nor too low to escape; and not until two in the morning, before an entranced audience that packed the tabernacle to the doors, did she complete her recital of the personal and detailed iniquities she knew of the community in which she had lived intimately all her days. Just as she was finishing, she remembered more.

"Huh!" she sniffed. "I gave last week one lot worth eight hundred dollars cash market price to Abel Ah Yo to pay running expenses and add up in Peter's books in heaven. Where did I get that lot? You all think Mr. Fleming Jason is a good man. He is more crooked than the entrance was to Pearl Lochs before the United States Government straightened the channel. He has liver disease now; but his sickness is a judgment of God, and he will die crooked. Mr. Fleming Jason gave me that lot twenty-two years ago, when its cash market price was thirty-five dollars. Because his aloha for me was big? No. He never had aloha inside of him except for dollars.

"You listen. Mr. Fleming Jason put a great sin upon me. When Frank Lomiloli was at my house, full of gin, for which gin Mr. Fleming Jason paid me in advance five times over, I got Frank Lomiloli to sign his name to the sale paper of his town land for one hundred dollars. It was worth six hundred then. It is worth twenty thousand now. Maybe you want to know where that town land is. I will tell you and remove it off my heart. It is on King Street, where is now the Come Again Saloon, the Japanese Taxicab Company garage, the Smith & Wilson plumbing shop, and the Ambrosia lee Cream Parlours, with the two more stories big Addison Lodging House overhead. And it is all wood, and always has been well painted. Yesterday they started painting it attain. But that paint will not stand between me and God. There are no more paint pots between me and my path to heaven."

The morning and evening papers of the day following held an unholy hush on the greatest news story of years; but Honolulu was half a-giggle and half aghast at the whispered reports, not always basely exaggerated, that circulated wherever two Honoluluans chanced to meet.

"Our mistake," said Colonel Chilton, at the club, "was that we did not, at the very first, appoint a committee of safety to keep track of Alice's soul."

Bob Cristy, one of the younger islanders, burst into laughter, so pointed and so loud that the meaning of it was demanded.

"Oh, nothing much," was his reply. "But I heard, on my way here, that old John Ward had just been run in for drunken and disorderly conduct and for resisting an officer. Now Abel Ah Yo fine-toothcombs the police court. He loves nothing better than soul-snatching a chronic drunkard."

Colonel Chilton looked at Lask Finneston, and both looked at Gary Wilkinson. He returned to them a similar look.

"The old beachcomber!" Lask Finneston cried. "The drunken old reprobate! I'd forgotten he was alive. Wonderful constitution. Never drew a sober breath except when he was shipwrecked, and, when I remember him, into every deviltry afloat. He must be going on eighty."

"He isn't far away from it," Bob Cristy nodded. "Still beach-combs, drinks when he gets the price, and keeps all his senses, though he's not spry and has to use glasses when he reads. And his memory is perfect. Now if Abel Ah Yo catches him . . . "

Gary Wilkinson cleared his throat preliminary to speech.

"Now there's a grand old man," he said. "A left-over from a forgotten age. Few of his type remain. A pioneer. A true kamaaina" (old-timer). "Helpless and in the hands of the police in his old age! We should do something for him in recognition of his yeoman work in Hawaii. His old home, I happen to know, is Sag Harbour. He hasn't seen it for over half a century. Now why shouldn't he be surprised to-morrow morning by having his fine paid, and by being presented with return tickets to Sag Harbour, and, say, expenses for a year's trip? I move a committee. I appoint Colonel Chilton, Lask Finneston, and . . . and myself. As for chairman, who more appropriate than Lask Finneston, who knew the old gentleman so well in the early days? Since there is no objection, I hereby appoint Lask Finneston chairman of the committee for the purpose of raising and donating money to pay the police-court fine and the expenses of a year's travel for that noble pioneer, John Ward, in recognition of a lifetime of devotion of energy to the upbuilding of Hawaii."

There was no dissent.

"The committee will now go into secret session," said Lask Finneston, arising and indicating the way to the library.

GLEN ELLEN, CALIFORNIA, August 30, 1916.

{1} See Dibble's "A History of the Sandwich Islands."

Shin-Bones

They have gone down to the pit with their weapons of war, and they have laid their swords under their heads.

"It was a sad thing to see the old lady revert."
Prince Akuli shot an apprehensive glance sideward to where, under the shade of a kukui tree, an old wahine (Hawaiian woman) was just settling herself to begin on some work in hand.
"Yes," he nodded half-sadly to me, "in her last years Hiwilani went back to the old ways, and to the old beliefs--in secret, of course. And, BELIEVE me, she was some collector herself. You should have seen her bones. She had them all about her bedroom, in big jars, and they constituted most all her relatives, except a half-dozen or so that Kanau beat her out of by getting to them first. The way the pair of them used to quarrel about those bones was awe- inspiring. And it gave me the creeps, when I was a boy, to go into that big, for-ever-twilight room of hers, and know that in this jar was all that remained of my maternal grand-aunt, and that in that jar was my great-grandfather, and that in all the jars were the preserved bone-remnants of the shadowy dust of the ancestors whose seed had come down and been incorporated in the living, breathing me. Hiwilani had gone quite native at the last, sleeping on mats on the hard floor--she'd fired out of the room the great, royal, canopied four-poster that had been presented to her grandmother by Lord Byron, who was the cousin of the Don Juan Byron and came here in the frigate Blonde in 1825.
"She went back to all native, at the last, and I can see her yet, biting a bite out of the raw fish ere she tossed them to her women to eat. And she made them finish her poi, or whatever else she did not finish of herself. She--"
But he broke off abruptly, and by the sensitive dilation of his nostrils and by the expression of his mobile features I saw that he had read in the air and identified the odour that offended him.
"Deuce take it!" he cried to me. "It stinks to heaven. And I shall be doomed to wear it until we're rescued."
There was no mistaking the object of his abhorrence. The ancient crone was making a dearest-loved lei (wreath) of the fruit of the hala which is the screw-pine or pandanus of the South Pacific. She was cutting the many sections or nut-envelopes of the fruit into fluted bell-shapes preparatory to stringing them on the twisted and tough inner bark of the hau tree. It certainly smelled to heaven, but, to me, a malahini (new-comer), the smell was wine-woody and fruit-juicy and not unpleasant.
Prince Akuli's limousine had broken an axle a quarter of a mile away, and he and I had sought shelter from the sun in this veritable bowery of a mountain home. Humble and grass-thatched was the house, but it stood in a treasure-garden of begonias that sprayed their delicate blooms a score of feet above our heads, that were like trees, with willowy trunks of trees as thick as a man's arm. Here we refreshed ourselves with drinking-coconuts, while a cowboy rode a dozen miles to the nearest telephone and summoned a machine from town. The town itself we could see, the Lakanaii metropolis of Olokona, a smudge of smoke on the shore-line, as we looked down across the miles of cane-fields, the billow-wreathed reef-lines, and the blue haze of ocean to where the island of Oahu shimmered like a dim opal on the horizon.
Maui is the Valley Isle of Hawaii, and Kauai the Garden Isle; but Lakanaii, lying abreast of Oahu, is recognized in the present, and was known of old and always, as the Jewel Isle of the

group. Not the largest, nor merely the smallest, Lakanaii is conceded by all to be the wildest, the most wildly beautiful, and, in its size, the richest of all the islands. Its sugar tonnage per acre is the highest, its mountain beef-cattle the fattest, its rainfall the most generous without ever being disastrous. It resembles Kauai in that it is the first-formed and therefore the oldest island, so that it had had time sufficient to break down its lava rock into the richest soil, and to erode the canyons between the ancient craters until they are like Grand Canyons of the Colorado, with numberless waterfalls plunging thousands of feet in the sheer or dissipating into veils of vapour, and evanescing in mid-air to descend softly and invisibly through a mirage of rainbows, like so much dew or gentle shower, upon the abyss-floors.

Yet Lakanaii is easy to describe. But how can one describe Prince Akuli? To know him is to know all Lakanaii most thoroughly. In addition, one must know thoroughly a great deal of the rest of the world. In the first place, Prince Akuli has no recognized nor legal right to be called "Prince." Furthermore, "Akuli" means the "squid." So that Prince Squid could scarcely be the dignified title of the straight descendant of the oldest and highest aliis (high chiefs) of Hawaii-- an old and exclusive stock, wherein, in the ancient way of the Egyptian Pharaohs, brothers and sisters had even wed on the throne for the reason that they could not marry beneath rank, that in all their known world there was none of higher rank, and that, at every hazard, the dynasty must be perpetuated.

I have heard Prince Akuli's singing historians (inherited from his father) chanting their interminable genealogies, by which they demonstrated that he was the highest alii in all Hawaii. Beginning with Wakea, who is their Adam, and with Papa, their Eve, through as many generations as there are letters in our alphabet they trace down to Nanakaoko, the first ancestor born in Hawaii and whose wife was Kahihiokalani. Later, but always highest, their generations split from the generations of Ua, who was the founder of the two distinct lines of the Kauai and Oahu kings.

In the eleventh century A.D., by the Lakanaii historians, at the time brothers and sisters mated because none existed to excel them, their rank received a boost of new blood of rank that was next to heaven's door. One Hoikemaha, steering by the stars and the ancient traditions, arrived in a great double-canoe from Samoa. He married a lesser alii of Lakanaii, and when his three sons were grown, returned with them to Samoa to bring back his own youngest brother. But with him he brought back Kumi, the son of Tui Manua, which latter's rank was highest in all Polynesia, and barely second to that of the demigods and gods. So the estimable seed of Kumi, eight centuries before, had entered into the aliis of Lakanaii, and been passed down by them in the undeviating line to reposit in Prince Akuli.

Him I first met, talking with an Oxford accent, in the officers' mess of the Black Watch in South Africa. This was just before that famous regiment was cut to pieces at Magersfontein. He had as much right to be in that mess as he had to his accent, for he was Oxford-educated and held the Queen's Commission. With him, as his guest, taking a look at the war, was Prince Cupid, so nicknamed, but the true prince of all Hawaii, including Lakanaii, whose real and legal title was Prince Jonah Kuhio Kalanianaole, and who might have been the living King of Hawaii Nei had it not been for the haole (white man) Revolution and Annexation--this, despite the fact that Prince Cupid's alii genealogy was lesser to the heaven-boosted genealogy of Prince Akuli. For Prince Akuli might have been King of Lakanaii, and of all Hawaii, perhaps, had not his grandfather been soundly thrashed by the first and greatest of the Kamehamehas.

This had occurred in the year 1810, in the booming days of the sandalwood trade, and in the same year that the King of Kauai came in, and was good, and ate out of Kamehameha's hand.

Prince Akuli's grandfather, in that year, had received his trouncing and subjugating because he was "old school." He had not imaged island empire in terms of gunpowder and haole gunners. Kamehameha, farther-visioned, had annexed the service of haoles, including such men as Isaac Davis, mate and sole survivor of the massacred crew of the schooner Fair American, and John Young, captured boatswain of the snow Eleanor. And Isaac Davis, and John Young, and others of their waywardly adventurous ilk, with six-pounder brass carronades from the captured Iphigenia and Fair American, had destroyed the war canoes and shattered the morale of the King of Lakanaii's land-fighters, receiving duly in return from Kamehameha, according to agreement: Isaac Davis, six hundred mature and fat hogs; John Young, five hundred of the same described pork on the hoof that was split.

And so, out of all incests and lusts of the primitive cultures and beast-man's gropings toward the stature of manhood, out of all red murders, and brute battlings, and matings with the younger brothers of the demigods, world-polished, Oxford-accented, twentieth century to the tick of the second, comes Prince Akuli, Prince Squid, pure-veined Polynesian, a living bridge across the thousand centuries, comrade, friend, and fellow-traveller out of his wrecked seven-thousand-dollar limousine, marooned with me in a begonia paradise fourteen hundred feet above the sea, and his island metropolis of Olokona, to tell me of his mother, who reverted in her old age to ancientness of religious concept and ancestor worship, and collected and surrounded herself with the charnel bones of those who had been her forerunners back in the darkness of time.

"King Kalakaua started this collecting fad, over on Oahu," Prince Akuli continued. "And his queen, Kapiolani, caught the fad from him. They collected everything--old makaloa mats, old tapas, old calabashes, old double-canoes, and idols which the priests had saved from the general destruction in 1819. I haven't seen a pearl-shell fish-hook in years, but I swear that Kalakaua accumulated ten thousand of them, to say nothing of human jaw-bone fish-hooks, and feather cloaks, and capes and helmets, and stone adzes, and poi-pounders of phallic design. When he and Kapiolani made their royal progresses around the islands, their hosts had to hide away their personal relics. For to the king, in theory, belongs all property of his people; and with Kalakaua, when it came to the old things, theory and practice were one.

"From him my father, Kanau, got the collecting bee in his bonnet, and Hiwilani was likewise infected. But father was modern to his finger-tips. He believed neither in the gods of the kahunas" (priests) "nor of the missionaries. He didn't believe in anything except sugar stocks, horse-breeding, and that his grandfather had been a fool in not collecting a few Isaac Davises and John Youngs and brass carronades before he went to war with Kamehameha. So he collected curios in the pure collector's spirit; but my mother took it seriously. That was why she went in for bones. I remember, too, she had an ugly old stone-idol she used to yammer to and crawl around on the floor before. It's in the Deacon Museum now. I sent it there after her death, and her collection of bones to the Royal Mausoleum in Olokona.

"I don't know whether you remember her father was Kaaukuu. Well, he was, and he was a giant. When they built the Mausoleum, his bones, nicely cleaned and preserved, were dug out of their hiding-place, and placed in the Mausoleum. Hiwilani had an old retainer, Ahuna. She stole the key from Kanau one night, and made Ahuna go and steal her father's bones out of the Mausoleum. I know. And he must have been a giant. She kept him in one of her big jars. One day, when I was a tidy size of a lad, and curious to know if Kaaukuu was as big as tradition had him, I fished his intact lower jaw out of the jar, and the wrappings, and tried it on. I stuck my head right through it, and it rested around my neck and on my shoulders like a horse collar. And every tooth was in the jaw, whiter than porcelain, without a cavity, the enamel unstained and unchipped. I got the walloping of my life for that offence, although she had to call old Ahuna in to help give it to me. But the incident served me well. It won her confidence in me that I was not afraid of the bones of the dead ones, and it won for me my Oxford education. As you shall see, if that car doesn't arrive first.

"Old Ahuna was one of the real old ones with the hall-mark on him and branded into him of faithful born-slave service. He knew more about my mother's family, and my father's, than did both of them put together. And he knew, what no living other knew, the burial- place of centuries, where were hid the bones of most of her ancestors and of Kanau's. Kanau couldn't worm it out of the old fellow, who looked upon Kanau as an apostate.

"Hiwilani struggled with the old codger for years. How she ever succeeded is beyond me. Of course, on the face of it, she was faithful to the old religion. This might have persuaded Ahuna to loosen up a little. Or she may have jolted fear into him; for she knew a lot of the line of chatter of the old Huni sorcerers, and she could make a noise like being on terms of utmost intimacy with Uli, who is the chiefest god of sorcery of all the sorcerers. She could skin the ordinary kahuna lapaau" (medicine man) "when it came to praying to Lonopuha and Koleamoku; read dreams and visions and signs and omens and indigestions to beat the band; make the practitioners under the medicine god, Maiola, look like thirty cents; pull off a pule hee incantation that would make them dizzy; and she claimed to a practice of kahuna hoenoho, which is modern spiritism, second to none. I have myself seen her drink the wind, throw a fit, and prophesy. The aumakuas were brothers to her when she slipped offerings to them across the altars of the ruined heiaus" (temples) "with a line of prayer that was as unintelligible to me as it was hair-raising. And as for old Ahuna, she could make him get down on the floor and yammer and bite himself when she pulled the real mystery dope on him.

"Nevertheless, my private opinion is that it was the anaana stuff that got him. She snipped off a lock of his hair one day with a pair of manicure scissors. This lock of hair was what we call the maunu, meaning the bait. And she took jolly good care to let him know she had that bit of his hair. Then she tipped it off to him that she had buried it, and was deeply engaged each night in her offerings and incantations to Uli."

"That was the regular praying-to-death?" I queried in the pause of Prince Akuli's lighting his cigarette.

"Sure thing," he nodded. "And Ahuna fell for it. First he tried to locate the hiding-place of the bait of his hair. Failing that, he hired a pahiuhiu sorcerer to find it for him. But Hiwilani queered that game by threatening to the sorcerer to practise apo leo on him, which is the art of permanently depriving a person of the power of speech without otherwise injuring him.

"Then it was that Ahuna began to pine away and get more like a corpse every day. In desperation he appealed to Kanau. I happened to be present. You have heard what sort of a man my father was.

"'Pig!' he called Ahuna. 'Swine-brains! Stinking fish! Die and be done with it. You are a fool. It is all nonsense. There is nothing in anything. The drunken haole, Howard, can prove the missionaries wrong. Square-face gin proves Howard wrong. The doctors say he won't last six months. Even square-face gin lies. Life is a liar, too. And here are hard times upon us, and a slump in sugar. Glanders has got into my brood mares. I wish I could lie down and sleep for a hundred years, and wake up to find sugar up a hundred points.'

"Father was something of a philosopher himself, with a bitter wit and a trick of spitting out staccato epigrams. He clapped his hands. 'Bring me a high-ball,' he commanded; 'no, bring me two high-balls.' Then he turned on Ahuna. 'Go and let yourself die, old heathen, survival of darkness, blight of the Pit that you are. But don't die on these premises. I desire merriment and laughter, and the sweet tickling of music, and the beauty of youthful motion, not the croaking of sick toads and googly-eyed corpses about me still afoot on their shaky legs. I'll be that way soon enough if I live long enough. And it will be my everlasting regret if I don't live long enough. Why in hell did I sink that last twenty thousand into Curtis's plantation? Howard warned me the slump was coming, but I thought it was the square-face making him lie. And Curtis has blown his brains out, and his head luna has run away with his daughter, and the sugar chemist has got typhoid, and everything's going to smash.'

"He clapped his hands for his servants, and commanded: 'Bring me my singing boys. And the hula dancers--plenty of them. And send for old Howard. Somebody's got to pay, and I'll shorten his six months of life by a month. But above all, music. Let there be music. It is stronger than drink, and quicker than opium.'

"He with his music druggery! It was his father, the old savage, who was entertained on board a French frigate, and for the first time heard an orchestra. When the little concert was over, the captain, to find which piece he liked best, asked which piece he'd like repeated. Well, when grandfather got done describing, what piece do you think it was?"

I gave up, while the Prince lighted a fresh cigarette.

"Why, it was the first one, of course. Not the real first one, but the tuning up that preceded it."

I nodded, with eyes and face mirthful of appreciation, and Prince Akuli, with another apprehensive glance at the old wahine and her half-made hala lei, returned to his tale of the bones of his ancestors.

"It was somewhere around this stage of the game that old Ahuna gave in to Hiwilani. He didn't exactly give in. He compromised. That's where I come in. If he would bring her the bones of her mother, and of her grandfather (who was the father of Kaaukuu, and who by tradition was rumoured to have been even bigger than his giant son, she would return to Ahuna the bait of his hair she was praying him to death with. He, on the other hand, stipulated that he was not to reveal to her the secret burial-place of all the alii of Lakanaii all the way back. Nevertheless, he was too old to dare the adventure alone, must be helped by some one who of necessity would come to know the secret, and I was that one. I was the highest alii, beside my father and mother, and they were no higher than I.

"So I came upon the scene, being summoned into the twilight room to confront those two dubious old ones who dealt with the dead. They were a pair--mother fat to despair of helplessness, Ahuna thin as a skeleton and as fragile. Of her one had the impression that if she lay down on her back she could not roll over without the aid of block-and-tackle; of Ahuna one's impression was that the tooth- pickedness of him would shatter to splinters if one bumped into him.

"And when they had broached the matter, there was more pilikia" (trouble). "My father's attitude stiffened my resolution. I refused to go on the bone-snatching expedition. I said I didn't care a whoop for the bones of all the aliis of my family and race. You see, I had just discovered Jules Verne, loaned me by old Howard, and was reading my head off. Bones? When there were North Poles, and Centres of Earths, and hairy comets to ride across space among the stars! Of course I didn't want to go on any bone- snatching expedition. I said my father was able-bodied, and he could go, splitting equally with her whatever bones he brought back. But she said he was only a blamed collector--or words to that effect, only stronger.

"'I know him,' she assured me. 'He'd bet his mother's bones on a horse-race or an ace-full.'

"I stood with fat her when it came to modern scepticism, and I told her the whole thing was rubbish. 'Bones?' I said. 'What are bones? Even field mice, and many rats, and cockroaches have bones, though the roaches wear their bones outside their meat instead of inside. The difference between man and other animals,' I told her, 'is not bones, but brain. Why, a bullock has bigger bones than a man, and more than one fish I've eaten has more bones, while a whale beats creation when it comes to bone.'

"It was frank talk, which is our Hawaiian way, as you have long since learned. In return, equally frank, she regretted she hadn't given me away as a feeding child when I was born. Next she bewailed that she had ever borne me. From that it was only a step to anaana me. She threatened me with it, and I did the bravest thing I have ever done. Old Howard had given me a knife of many blades, and corkscrews, and screw-drivers, and all sorts of contrivances, including a tiny pair of scissors. I proceeded to pare my finger-nails.

"'There,' I said, as I put the parings into her hand. 'Just to show you what I think of it. There's bait and to spare. Go on and anaana me if you can.'

"I have said it was brave. It was. I was only fifteen, and I had lived all my days in the thick of the mystery stuff, while my scepticism, very recently acquired, was only skin-deep. I could be a sceptic out in the open in the sunshine. But I was afraid of the dark. And in that twilight room, the bones of the dead all about me in the big jars, why, the old lady had me scared stiff. As we say to-day, she had my goat. Only I was brave and didn't let on. And I put my bluff across, for my mother flung the parings into my face and burst into tears. Tears in an elderly woman weighing three hundred and twenty pounds are scarcely impressive, and I hardened the brassiness of my bluff.

"She shifted her attack, and proceeded to talk with the dead. Nay, more, she summoned them there, and, though I was all ripe to see but couldn't, Ahuna saw the father of Kaaukuu in the corner and lay down on the floor and yammered. Just the same, although I almost saw the old giant, I didn't quite see him.

"'Let him talk for himself,' I said. But Hiwilani persisted in doing the talking for him, and in laying upon me his solemn injunction that I must go with Ahuna to the burial-place and bring back the bones desired by my mother. But I argued that if the dead ones could be invoked to kill living men by wasting sicknesses, and that if the dead ones could transport themselves from their burial- crypts into the corner of her room, I couldn't see why they shouldn't leave their bones behind them, there in her room and ready to be jarred, when they said good-bye and departed for the middle world, the over world, or the under world, or wherever thcy abided when they weren't paying social calls.

"Whereupon mother let loose on poor old Ahuna, or let loose upon him the ghost of Kaaukuu's father, supposed to be crouching there in the corner, who commanded Ahuna to divulge to her the burial- place. I tried to stiffen him up, telling him to let the old ghost divulge the secret himself, than whom nobody else knew it better, seeing that he had resided there upwards of a century. But Ahuna was old school. He possessed no iota of scepticism. The more Hiwilani frightened him, the more he rolled on the floor and the louder he yammered.

"But when he began to bite himself, I gave in. I felt sorry for him; but, over and beyond that, I began to admire him. He was sterling stuff, even if he was a survival of darkness. Here, with the fear of mystery cruelly upon him, believing Hiwilani's dope implicitly, he was caught between two fidelities. She was his living alii, his alii kapo" (sacred chiefess). "He must be faithful to her, yet more faithful must he be to all the dead and gone aliis of her line who depended solely on him that their bones should not be disturbed.

"I gave in. But I, too, imposed stipulations. Steadfastly had my father, new school, refused to let me go to England for my education. That sugar was slumping was reason sufficient for him. Steadfastly had my mother, old school, refused, her heathen mind too dark to place any value on education, while it was shrewd enough to discern that education led to unbelief in all that was old. I wanted to study, to study science, the arts, philosophy, to study everything old Howard knew, which enabled him, on the edge of the grave, undauntedly to sneer at superstition, and to give me Jules Verne to read. He was an Oxford man before he went wild and wrong, and it was he who had set the Oxford bee buzzing in my noddle.

"In the end Ahuna and I, old school and new school leagued together, won out. Mother promised that she'd make father send me to England, even if she had to pester him into a prolonged drinking that would make his digestion go back on him. Also, Howard was to accompany me, so that I could decently bury him in England. He was a queer one, old Howard, an individual if there ever was one. Let me tell you a little story about him. It was when Kalakaua was starting on his trip around the world. You remember, when Armstrong, and Judd, and the drunken valet of a German baron accompanied him. Kalakaua made the proposition to Howard . . . "

But here the long-apprehended calamity fell upon Prince Akuli. The old wahine had finished her lei hala. Barefooted, with no adornment of femininity, clad in a shapeless shift of much-washed cotton, with age-withered face and labour-gnarled hands, she cringed before him and crooned a mele in his honour, and, still cringing, put the lei around his neck. It is true the hala smelled most freshly strong, yet was the act beautiful to me, and the old woman herself beautiful to me. My mind leapt into the Prince's narrative so that to Ahuna I could not help likening her.

Oh, truly, to be an alii in Hawaii, even in this second decade of the twentieth century, is no light thing. The alii, utterly of the new, must be kindly and kingly to those old ones absolutely of the old. Nor did the Prince without a kingdom, his loved island long since annexed by the United States and incorporated into a territory along with the rest of the Hawaiian Islands--nor did the Prince betray his repugnance for the odour of the hala. He bowed his head graciously; and his royal condescending words of pure Hawaiian I knew would make the old woman's heart warm until she died with remembrance of the wonderful occasion. The wry grimace he stole to me would not have been made had he felt any uncertainty of its escaping her.

"And so," Prince Akuli resumed, after the wahine had tottered away in an ecstasy, "Ahuna and I departed on our grave-robbing adventure. You know the Iron-bound Coast."

I nodded, knowing full well the spectacle of those lava leagues of weather coast, truly iron-bound so far as landing-places or anchorages were concerned, great forbidding cliff-walls thousands of feet in height, their summits wreathed in cloud and rain squall, their knees hammered by the trade-wind billows into spouting, spuming white, the air, from sea to rain-cloud, spanned by a myriad leaping waterfalls, provocative, in day or night, of countless sun and lunar rainbows. Valleys, so called, but fissures rather, slit the cyclopean walls here and there, and led away into a lofty and madly vertical back country, most of it inaccessible to the foot of man and trod only by the wild goat.

"Precious little you know of it," Prince Akuli retorted, in reply to my nod. "You've seen it only from the decks of steamers. There are valleys there, inhabited valleys, out of which there is no exit by land, and perilously accessible by canoe only on the selected days of two months in the year. When I was twenty-eight I was over there in one of them on a hunting trip. Bad weather, in the auspicious period, marooned us for three weeks. Then five of my party and myself swam for it out through the surf. Three of us made the canoes waiting for us. The other two were flung back on the sand, each with a broken arm. Save for us, the entire party remained there until the next year, ten months afterward. And one of them was Wilson, of Wilson & Wall, the Honolulu sugar factors. And he was engaged to be married.

"I've seen a goat, shot above by a hunter above, land at my feet a thousand yards underneath. BELIEVE me, that landscape seemed to rain goats and rocks for ten minutes. One of my canoemen fell off the trail between the two little valleys of Aipio and Luno. He hit first fifteen hundred feet beneath us, and fetched up in a ledge three hundred feet farther down. We didn't bury him. We couldn't get to him, and flying machines had not yet been invented. His bones are there now, and, barring earthquake and volcano, will be there when the Trumps of Judgment sound.

"Goodness me! Only the other day, when our Promotion Committee, trying to compete with Honolulu for the tourist trade, called in the engineers to estimate what it would cost to build a scenic drive around the Iron-bound Coast, the lowest figures were a quarter of a million dollars a mile!

"And Ahuna and I, an old man and a young boy, started for that stern coast in a canoe paddled by old men! The youngest of them, the steersman, was over sixty, while the rest of them averaged seventy at the very least. There were eight of them, and we started in the night-time, so that none should see us go. Even these old ones, trusted all their lives, knew no more than the fringe of the secret. To the fringe, only, could they take us.

"And the fringe was--I don't mind telling that much--the fringe was Ponuloo Valley. We got there the third afternoon following. The old chaps weren't strong on the paddles. It was a funny expedition, into such wild waters, with now one and now another of our ancient-mariner crew collapsing and even fainting. One of them actually died on the second morning out. We buried him overside. It was positively uncanny, the heathen ceremonies those grey ones pulled off in burying their grey brother. And I was only fifteen, alii kapo over them by blood of heathenness and right of hereditary heathen rule, with a penchant for Jules Verne and shortly to sail for England for my education! So one learns. Small wonder my father was a philosopher, in his own lifetime spanning the history of man from human sacrifice and idol worship, through the religions of man's upward striving, to the Medusa of rank atheism at the end of it all. Small wonder that, like old Ecclesiastes, he found vanity in all things and surcease in sugar stocks, singing boys, and hula dancers."

Prince Akuli debated with his soul for an interval.

"Oh, well," he sighed, "I have done some spanning of time myself." He sniffed disgustedly of the odour of the hala lei that stifled him. "It stinks of the ancient." he vouchsafed. "I? I stink of the modern. My father was right. The sweetest of all is sugar up a hundred points, or four aces in a poker game. If the Big War lasts another year, I shall clean up three-quarters of a million over a million. If peace breaks to-morrow, with the consequent slump, I could enumerate a hundred who will lose my direct bounty, and go into the old natives' homes my father and I long since endowed for them."

He clapped his hands, and the old wahine tottered toward him in an excitement of haste to serve. She cringed before him, as he drew pad and pencil from his breast pocket.

"Each month, old woman of our old race," he addressed her, "will you receive, by rural free delivery, a piece of written paper that you can exchange with any storekeeper anywhere for ten dollars gold. This shall be so for as long as you live. Behold! I write the record and the remembrance of it, here and now, with this pencil on this paper. And this is because you are of my race and service, and because you have honoured me this day with your mats to sit upon and your thrice-blessed and thrice-delicious lei hala."

He turned to me a weary and sceptical eye, saying:

"And if I die to-morrow, not alone will the lawyers contest my disposition of my property, but they will contest my benefactions and my pensions accorded, and the clarity of my mind.

"It was the right weather of the year; but even then, with our old weak ones at the paddles, we did not attempt the landing until we had assembled half the population of Ponuloo Valley down on the steep little beach. Then we counted our waves, selected the best one, and ran in on it. Of course, the canoe was swamped and the outrigger smashed, but the ones on shore dragged us up unharmed beyond the wash.

"Ahuna gave his orders. In the night-time all must remain within their houses, and the dogs be tied up and have their jaws bound so that there should be no barking. And in the night-time Ahuna and I stole out on our journey, no one knowing whether we went to the right or left or up the valley toward its head. We carried jerky, and hard poi and dried aku, and from the quantity of the food I knew we were to be gone several days. Such a trail! A Jacob's ladder to the sky, truly, for that first pali" (precipice), "almost straight up, was three thousand feet above the sea. And we did it in the dark!

"At the top, beyond the sight of the valley we had left, we slept until daylight on the hard rock in a hollow nook Ahuna knew, and that was so small that we were squeezed. And the old fellow, for fear that I might move in the heavy restlessness of lad's sleep, lay on the outside with one arm resting across me. At daybreak, I saw why. Between us and the lip of the cliff scarcely a yard intervened. I crawled to the lip and looked, watching the abyss take on immensity in the growing light and trembling from the fear of height that was upon me. At last I made out the sea, over half a mile straight beneath. And we had done this thing in the dark!

"Down in the next valley, which was a very tiny one, we found evidence of the ancient population, but there were no people. The only way was the crazy foot-paths up and down the dizzy valley walls from valley to valley. But lean and aged as Ahuna was, he seemed untirable. In the second valley dwelt an old leper in hiding. He did not know me, and when Ahuna told him who I was, he grovelled at my feet, almost clasping them, and mumbled a mele of all my line out of a lipless mouth.

"The next valley proved to be the valley. It was long and so narrow that its floor had caught not sufficient space of soil to grow taro for a single person. Also, it had no beach, the stream that threaded it leaping a pali of several hundred feet down to the sea. It was a god-forsaken place of naked, eroded lava, to which only rarely could the scant vegetation find root-hold. For miles we followed up that winding fissure through the towering walls, far into the chaos of back country that lies behind the Iron-bound Coast. How far that valley penetrated I do not know, but, from the quantity of water in the stream, I judged it far. We did not go to the valley's head. I could see Ahuna casting glances to all the peaks, and I knew he was taking bearings, known to him alone, from natural objects. When he halted at the last, it was with abrupt certainty. His bearings had crossed. He threw down the portion of food and outfit he had carried. It was the place. I looked on either hand at the hard, implacable walls, naked of vegetation, and could dream of no burial-place possible in such bare adamant.

"We ate, then stripped for work. Only did Ahuna permit me to retain my shoes. He stood beside me at the edge of a deep pool, likewise apparelled and prodigiously skinny.

"'You will dive down into the pool at this spot,' he said. 'Search the rock with your hands as you descend, and, about a fathom and a half down, you will find a hole. Enter it, head-first, but going slowly, for the lava rock is sharp and may cut your head and body.'

"'And then?' I queried. 'You will find the hole growing larger,' was his answer. 'When you have gone all of eight fathoms along the passage, come up slowly, and you will find your head in the air, above water, in the dark. Wait there then for me. The water is very cold.'

"It didn't sound good to me. I was thinking, not of the cold water and the dark, but of the bones. 'You go first,' I said. But he claimed he could not. 'You are my alii, my prince,' he said. 'It is impossible that I should go before you into the sacred burial- place of your kingly ancestors.'

"But the prospect did not please. 'Just cut out this prince stuff,' I told him. 'It isn't what it's cracked up to be. You go first, and I'll never tell on you.' 'Not alone the living must we please,' he admonished, 'but, more so, the dead must we please. Nor can we lie to the dead.'

"We argued it out, and for half an hour it was stalemate. I wouldn't, and he simply couldn't. He tried to buck me up by appealing to my pride. He chanted the heroic deeds of my ancestors; and, I remember especially, he sang to me of Mokomoku, my great-grandfather and the gigantic father of the gigantic Kaaukuu, telling how thrice in battle Mokomoku leaped among his foes, seizing by the neck a warrior in either hand and knocking their heads together until they were dead. But this was not what decided me. I really felt sorry for old Ahuna, he was so beside himself for fear the expedition would come to naught. And I was coming to a great admiration for the old fellow, not least among the reasons being the fact of his lying down to sleep between me and the cliff-lip.

"So, with true alii-authority of command, saying, 'You will immediately follow after me,' I dived in. Everything he had said was correct. I found the entrance to the subterranean passage, swam carefully through it, cutting my shoulder once on the lava- sharp roof, and emerged in the darkness and air. But before I could count thirty, he broke water beside me, rested his hand on my arm to make sure of me, and directed me to swim ahead of him for the matter of a hundred feet or so. Then we touched bottom and climbed out on the rocks. And still no light, and I remember I was glad that our altitude was too high for centipedes.

"He had brought with him a coconut calabash, tightly stoppered, of whale-oil that must have been landed on Lahaina beach thirty years before. From his mouth he took a water-tight arrangement of a matchbox composed of two empty rifle-cartridges fitted snugly together. He lighted the wicking that floated on the oil, and I looked about, and knew disappointment. No burial-chamber was it, but merely a lava tube such as occurs on all the islands.

"He put the calabash of light into my hands and started me ahead of him on the way, which he assured me was long, but not too long. It was long, at least a mile in my sober judgment, though at the time it seemed five miles; and it ascended sharply. When Ahuna, at the last, stopped me, I knew we were close to our goal. He knelt on his lean old knees on the sharp lava rock, and clasped my knees with his skinny arms. My hand that was free of the calabash lamp he placed on his head. He chanted to me, with his old cracked, quavering voice, the line of my descent and my essential high alii- ness. And then he said:

"'Tell neither Kanau nor Hiwilani aught of what you are about to behold. There is no sacredness in Kanau. His mind is filled with sugar and the breeding of horses. I do know that he sold a feather cloak his grandfather had worn to that English collector for eight thousand dollars, and the money he lost the next day betting on the polo game between Maui and Oahu. Hiwilani, your mother, is filled with sacredness. She is too much filled with sacredness. She grows old, and weak-headed, and she traffics over-much with sorceries.'

"'No,' I made answer. 'I shall tell no one. If I did, then would I have to return to this place again. And I do not want ever to return to this place. I'll try anything once. This I shall never try twice.'

"'It is well,' he said, and arose, falling behind so that I should enter first. Also, he said: 'Your mother is old. I shall bring her, as promised, the bones of her mother and of her grandfather. These should content her until she dies; and then, if I die before her, it is you who must see to it that all the bones in her family collection are placed in the Royal Mausoleum.'

"I have given all the Islands' museums the once-over," Prince Akuli lapsed back into slang, "and I must say that the totality of the collections cannot touch what I saw in our Lakanaii burial-cave. Remember, and with reason and history, we trace back the highest and oldest genealogy in the Islands. Everything that I had ever dreamed or heard of, and much more that I had not, was there. The place was wonderful. Ahuna, sepulchrally muttering prayers and meles, moved about, lighting various whale-oil lamp-calabashes. They were all there, the Hawaiian race from the beginning of Hawaiian time. Bundles of bones and bundles of bones, all wrapped decently in tapa, until for all the world it was like the parcels- post department at a post office.

"And everything! Kahilis, which you may know developed out of the fly-flapper into symbols of royalty until they became larger than hearse-plumes with handles a fathom and a half and over two fathoms in length. And such handles! Of the wood of the kauila, inlaid with shell and ivory and bone with a cleverness that had died out among our artificers a century before. It was a centuries-old family attic. For the first time I saw things I had only heard of, such as the pahoas, fashioned of whale-teeth and suspended by braided human hair, and worn on the breast only by the highest of rank.

"There were tapes and mats of the rarest and oldest; capes and leis and helmets and cloaks, priceless all, except the too-ancient ones, of the feathers of the mamo, and of the iwi and the akakane and the o-o. I saw one of the mamo cloaks that was superior to that finest one in the Bishop Museum in Honolulu, and that they value at between half a million and a million dollars. Goodness me, I thought at the time, it was lucky Kanau didn't know about it.

"Such a mess of things! Carved gourds and calabashes, shell- scrapers, nets of olona fibre, a junk of ie-ie baskets, and fish- hooks of every bone and spoon of shell. Musical instruments of the forgotten days--ukukes and nose flutes, and kiokios which are likewise played with one unstopped nostril. Taboo poi bowls and finger bowls, left-handed adzes of the canoe gods, lava-cup lamps, stone mortars and pestles and poi-pounders. And adzes again, a myriad of them, beautiful ones, from an ounce in weight for the finer carving of idols to fifteen pounds for the felling of trees, and all with the sweetest handles I have ever beheld.

"There were the kaekeekes--you know, our ancient drums, hollowed sections of the coconut tree, covered one end with shark-skin. The first kaekeeke of all Hawaii Ahuna pointed out to me and told me the tale. It was manifestly most ancient. He was afraid to touch it for fear the age-rotted wood of it would crumble to dust, the ragged tatters of the shark-skin head of it still attached. 'This is the very oldest and father of all our kaekeekes,' Ahuna told me. 'Kila, the son of Moikeha, brought it back from far Raiatea in the South Pacific. And it was Kila's own son, Kahai, who made that same journey, and was gone ten years, and brought back with him from Tahiti the first breadfruit trees that sprouted and grew on Hawaiian soil.'

"And the bones and bones! The parcel-delivery array of them! Besides the small bundles of the long bones, there were full skeletons, tapa-wrapped, lying in one-man, and two- and three-man canoes of precious koa wood, with curved outriggers of wiliwili wood, and proper paddles to hand with the io-projection at the point simulating the continuance of the handle, as if, like a skewer, thrust through the flat length of the blade. And their war weapons were laid away by the sides of the lifeless bones that had wielded them--rusty old horse-pistols, derringers, pepper-boxes, five-barrelled fantastiques, Kentucky long riffles, muskets handled in trade by John Company and Hudson's Bay, shark-tooth swords, wooden stabbing-knives, arrows and spears bone-headed of the fish and the pig and of man, and spears and arrows wooden-headed and fire-hardened.

"Ahuna put a spear in my hand, headed and pointed finely with the long shin-bone of a man, and told me the tale of it. But first he unwrapped the long bones, arms, and legs, of two parcels, the bones, under the wrappings, neatly tied like so many faggots. 'This,' said Ahuna, exhibiting the pitiful white contents of one parcel, 'is Laulani. She was the wife of Akaiko, whose bones, now placed in your hands, much larger and male-like as you observe, held up the flesh of a large man, a three-hundred pounder seven- footer, three centuries agone. And this spear-head is made of the shin-bone of Keola, a mighty wrestler and runner of their own time and place. And he loved Laulani, and she fled with him. But in a forgotten battle on the sands of Kalini, Akaiko rushed the lines of the enemy, leading the charge that was successful, and seized upon Keola, his wife's lover, and threw him to the ground, and sawed through his neck to the death with a shark-tooth knife. Thus, in the old days as always, did man combat for woman with man. And Laulani was beautiful; that Keola should be made into a spearhead for her! She was formed like a queen, and her body was a long bowl of sweetness, and her fingers lomi'd' (massaged) 'to slimness and smallness at her mother's breast. For ten generations have we remembered her beauty. Your father's singing boys to-day sing of her beauty in the hula that is named of her! This is Laulani, whom you hold in your hands.'

"And, Ahuna done, I could but gaze, with imagination at the one time sobered and fired. Old drunken Howard had lent me his Tennyson, and I had mooned long and often over the Idyls of the King. Here were the three, I thought--Arthur, and Launcelot, and Guinevere. This, then, I pondered, was the end of it all, of life and strife and striving and love, the weary spirits of these long- gone ones to be invoked by fat old women and mangy sorcerers, the bones of them to be esteemed of collectors and betted on horse- races and ace-fulls or to be sold for cash and invested in sugar stocks.

"For me it was illumination. I learned there in the burial-cave the great lesson. And to Ahuna I said: 'The spear headed with the long bone of Keola I shall take for my own. Never shall I sell it. I shall keep it always.'

"'And for what purpose?' he demanded. And I replied: 'That the contemplation of it may keep my hand sober and my feet on earth with the knowledge that few men are fortunate enough to have as much of a remnant of themselves as will compose a spearhead when they are three centuries dead.'

"And Ahuna bowed his head, and praised my wisdom of judgment. But at that moment the long-rotted olona-cord broke and the pitiful woman's bones of Laulani shed from my clasp and clattered on the rocky floor. One shin-bone, in some way deflected, fell under the dark shadow of a canoe-bow, and I made up my mind that it should be mine. So I hastened to help him in the picking up of the bones and the tying, so that he did not notice its absence.

"'This,' said Ahuna, introducing me to another of my ancestors, 'is your great-grandfather, Mokomoku, the father of Kaaukuu. Behold the size of his bones. He was a giant. I shall carry him, because of the long spear of Keola that will be difficult for you to carry away. And this is Lelemahoa, your grandmother, the mother of your mother, that you shall carry. And day grows short, and we must still swim up through the waters to the sun ere darkness hides the sun from the world.'

"But Ahuna, putting out the various calabashes of light by drowning the wicks in the whale-oil, did not observe me include the shinbone of Laulani with the bones of my grandmother."

The honk of the automobile, sent up from Olokona to rescue us, broke off the Prince's narrative. We said good-bye to the ancient and fresh-pensioned wahine, and departed. A half-mile on our way, Prince Akuli resumed.

"So Ahuna and I returned to Hiwilani, and to her happiness, lasting to her death the year following, two more of her ancestors abided about her in the jars of her twilight room. Also, she kept her compact and worried my father into sending me to England. I took old Howard along, and he perked up and confuted the doctors, so that it was three years before I buried him restored to the bosom of my family. Sometimes I think he was the most brilliant man I have ever known. Not until my return from England did Ahuna die, the last custodian of our alii secrets. And at his death-bed he pledged me again never to reveal the location in that nameless valley, and never to go back myself.

"Much else I have forgotten to mention did I see there in the cave that one time. There were the bones of Kumi, the near demigod, son of Tui Manua of Samoa, who, in the long before, married into my line and heaven-boosted my genealogy. And the bones of my great-grandmother who had slept in the four-poster presented her by Lord Byron. And Ahuna hinted tradition that there was reason for that presentation, as well as for the historically known lingering of the Blonde in Olokona for so long. And I held her poor bones in my hands--bones once fleshed with sensate beauty, informed with sparkle and spirit, instinct with love and love-warmness of arms around and eyes and lips together, that had begat me in the end of the generations unborn. It was a good experience. I am modern, 'tis true. I believe in no mystery stuff of old time nor of the kahunas. And yet, I saw in that cave things which I dare not name to you, and which I, since old Ahuna died, alone of the living know. I have no children. With me my long line ceases. This is the twentieth century, and we stink of gasolene. Nevertheless these other and nameless things shall die with me. I shall never revisit the burial-place. Nor in all time to come will any man gaze upon it through living eyes unless the quakes of earth rend the mountains asunder and spew forth the secrets contained in the hearts of the mountains."

Prince Akuli ceased from speech. With welcome relief on his face, he removed the lei hala from his neck, and, with a sniff and a sigh, tossed it into concealment in the thick lantana by the side of the road.

"But the shin-bone of Laulani?" I queried softly.

He remained silent while a mile of pasture land fled by us and yielded to caneland.

"I have it now," he at last said. "And beside it is Keola, slain ere his time and made into a spear-head for love of the woman whose shin-bone abides near to him. To them, those poor pathetic bones, I owe more than to aught else. I became possessed of them in the period of my culminating adolescence. I know they changed the entire course of my life and trend of my mind. They gave to me a modesty and a humility in the world, from which my father's fortune has ever failed to seduce me.

"And often, when woman was nigh to winning to the empery of my mind over me, I sought Laulani's shin-bone. And often, when lusty manhood stung me into feeling over-proud and lusty, I consulted the spearhead remnant of Keola, one-time swift runner, and mighty wrestler and lover, and thief of the wife of a king. The contemplation of them has ever been of profound aid to me, and you might well say that I have founded my religion or practice of living upon them."

WAIKIKI, HONOLULU, HAWAIIAN ISLANDS. July 16, 1916.

The Water Baby

I lent a weary ear to old Kohokumu's interminable chanting of the deeds and adventures of Maui, the Promethean demi-god of Polynesia who fished up dry land from ocean depths with hooks made fast to heaven, who lifted up the sky whereunder previously men had gone on all-fours, not having space to stand erect, and who made the sun with its sixteen snared legs stand still and agree thereafter to traverse the sky more slowly--the sun being evidently a trade unionist and believing in the six-hour day, while Maui stood for the open shop and the twelve-hour day.

"Now this," said Kohokumu, "is from Queen Lililuokalani's own family mele:

"Maui became restless and fought the sun With a noose that he laid. And winter won the sun, And summer was won by Maui . . . "

Born in the Islands myself, I knew the Hawaiian myths better than this old fisherman, although I possessed not his memorization that enabled him to recite them endless hours.

"And you believe all this?" I demanded in the sweet Hawaiian tongue.

"It was a long time ago," he pondered. "I never saw Maui with my own eyes. But all our old men from all the way back tell us these things, as I, an old man, tell them to my sons and grandsons, who will tell them to their sons and grandsons all the way ahead to come."

"You believe," I persisted, "that whopper of Maui roping the sun like a wild steer, and that other whopper of heaving up the sky from off the earth?"

"I am of little worth, and am not wise, O Lakana," my fisherman made answer. "Yet have I read the Hawaiian Bible the missionaries translated to us, and there have I read that your Big Man of the Beginning made the earth, and sky, and sun, and moon, and stars, and all manner of animals from horses to cockroaches and from centipedes and mosquitoes to sea lice and jellyfish, and man and woman, and everything, and all in six days. Why, Maui didn't do anything like that much. He didn't make anything. He just put things in order, that was all, and it took him a long, long time to make the improvements. And anyway, it is much easier and more reasonable to believe the little whopper than the big whopper."

And what could I reply? He had me on the matter of reasonableness. Besides, my head ached. And the funny thing, as I admitted it to myself, was that evolution teaches in no uncertain voice that man did run on all-fours ere he came to walk upright, that astronomy states flatly that the speed of the revolution of the earth on its axis has diminished steadily, thus increasing the length of day, and that the seismologists accept that all the islands of Hawaii were elevated from the ocean floor by volcanic action.

Fortunately, I saw a bamboo pole, floating on the surface several hundred feet away, suddenly up-end and start a very devil's dance. This was a diversion from the profitless discussion, and Kohokumu and I dipped our paddles and raced the little outrigger canoe to the dancing pole. Kohokumu caught the line that was fast to the butt of the pole and under-handed it in until a two-foot ukikiki, battling fiercely to the end, flashed its wet silver in the sun and began beating a tattoo on the inside bottom of the canoe. Kohokumu picked up a squirming, slimy squid, with his teeth bit a chunk of live bait out of it, attached the bait to the hook, and dropped line and sinker overside. The stick floated flat on the surface of the water, and the canoe drifted slowly away. With a survey of the crescent composed of a score of such sticks all lying flat, Kohokumu wiped his hands on his naked sides and lifted the wearisome and centuries-old chant of Kuali:

"Oh, the great fish-hook of Maui! Manai-i-ka-lani--"made fast to the heavens"! An earth-twisted cord ties the hook, Engulfed from lofty Kauiki! Its bait the red-billed Alae, The bird to Hina sacred! It sinks far down to Hawaii, Struggling and in pain dying! Caught is the land beneath the water, Floated up, up to the surface, But Hina hid a wing of the bird And broke the land beneath the water! Below was the bait snatched away And eaten at once by the fishes, The Ulua of the deep muddy places!

His aged voice was hoarse and scratchy from the drinking of too much swipes at a funeral the night before, nothing of which contributed to make me less irritable. My head ached. The sun-glare on the water made my eyes ache, while I was suffering more than half a touch of mal de mer from the antic conduct of the outrigger on the blobby sea. The air was stagnant. In the lee of Waihee, between the white beach and the roof, no whisper of breeze eased the still sultriness. I really think I was too miserable to summon the resolution to give up the fishing and go in to shore.

Lying back with closed eyes, I lost count of time. I even forgot that Kohokumu was chanting till reminded of it by his ceasing. An exclamation made me bare my eyes to the stab of the sun. He was gazing down through the water-glass.

"It's a big one," he said, passing me the device and slipping over- side feet-first into the water.

He went under without splash and ripple, turned over and swam down. I followed his progress through the water-glass, which is merely an oblong box a couple of feet long, open at the top, the bottom sealed water-tight with a sheet of ordinary glass.

Now Kohokumu was a bore, and I was squeamishly out of sorts with him for his volubleness, but I could not help admiring him as I watched him go down. Past seventy years of age, lean as a toothpick, and shrivelled like a mummy, he was doing what few young athletes of my race would do or could do. It was forty feet to bottom. There, partly exposed, but mostly hidden under the bulge of a coral lump, I could discern his objective. His keen eyes had caught the projecting tentacle of a squid. Even as he swam, the tentacle was lazily withdrawn, so that there was no sign of the creature. But the brief exposure of the portion of one tentacle had advertised its owner as a squid of size.

The pressure at a depth of forty feet is no joke for a young man, yet it did not seem to inconvenience this oldster. I am certain it never crossed his mind to be inconvenienced. Unarmed, bare of body save for a brief malo or loin cloth, he was undeterred by the formidable creature that constituted his prey. I saw him steady himself with his right hand on the coral lump, and thrust his left arm into the hole to the shoulder. Half a minute elapsed, during which time he seemed to be groping and rooting around with his left hand. Then tentacle after tentacle, myriad-suckered and wildly waving, emerged. Laying hold of his arm, they writhed and coiled about his flesh like so many snakes. With a heave and a jerk appeared the entire squid, a proper devil-fish or octopus.

But the old man was in no hurry for his natural element, the air above the water. There, forty feet beneath, wrapped about by an octopus that measured nine feet across from tentacle-tip to tentacle-tip and that could well drown the stoutest swimmer, he coolly and casually did the one thing that gave to him and his empery over the monster. He shoved his lean, hawk-like face into the very centre of the slimy, squirming mass, and with his several ancient fangs bit into the heart and the life of the matter. This accomplished, he came upward, slowly, as a swimmer should who is changing atmospheres from the depths. Alongside the canoe, still in the water and peeling off the grisly clinging thing, the incorrigible old sinner burst into the pule of triumph which had been chanted by the countless squid-catching generations before him:

"O Kanaloa of the taboo nights! Stand upright on the solid floor! Stand upon the floor where lies the squid! Stand up to take the squid of the deep sea! Rise up, O Kanaloa! Stir up! Stir up! Let the squid awake! Let the squid that lies flat awake! Let the squid that lies spread out . . . "

I closed my eyes and ears, not offering to lend him a hand, secure in the knowledge that he could climb back unaided into the unstable craft without the slightest risk of upsetting it.

"A very fine squid," he crooned. "It is a wahine" (female) "squid. I shall now sing to you the song of the cowrie shell, the red cowrie shell that we used as a bait for the squid--"

"You were disgraceful last night at the funeral," I headed him off. "I heard all about it. You made much noise. You sang till everybody was deaf. You insulted the son of the widow. You drank swipes like a pig. Swipes are not good for your extreme age. Some day you will wake up dead. You ought to be a wreck to-day--"

"Ha!" he chuckled. "And you, who drank no swipes, who was a babe unborn when I was already an old man, who went to bed last night with the sun and the chickens--this day are you a wreck. Explain me that. My ears are as thirsty to listen as was my throat thirsty last night. And here to-day, behold, I am, as that Englishman who came here in his yacht used to say, I am in fine form, in devilish fine form."

"I give you up," I retorted, shrugging my shoulders. "Only one thing is clear, and that is that the devil doesn't want you. Report of your singing has gone before you."

"No," he pondered the idea carefully. "It is not that. The devil will be glad for my coming, for I have some very fine songs for him, and scandals and old gossips of the high aliis that will make him scratch his sides. So, let me explain to you the secret of my birth. The Sea is my mother. I was born in a double-canoe, during a Kona gale, in the channel of Kahoolawe. From her, the Sea, my mother, I received my strength. Whenever I return to her arms, as for a breast-clasp, as I have returned this day, I grow strong again and immediately. She, to me, is the milk-giver, the life- source--"

"Shades of Antaeus!" thought I.

"Some day," old Kohokumu rambled on, "when I am really old, I shall be reported of men as drowned in the sea. This will be an idle thought of men. In truth, I shall have returned into the arms of my mother, there to rest under the heart of her breast until the second birth of me, when I shall emerge into the sun a flashing youth of splendour like Maui himself when he was golden young."

"A queer religion," I commented.

"When I was younger I muddled my poor head over queerer religions," old Kohokumu retorted. "But listen, O Young Wise One, to my elderly wisdom. This I know: as I grow old I seek less for the truth from without me, and find more of the truth from within me. Why have I thought this thought of my return to my mother and of my rebirth from my mother into the sun? You do not know. I do not know, save that, without whisper of man's voice or printed word, without prompting from otherwhere, this thought has arisen from within me, from the deeps of me that are as deep as the sea. I am not a god. I do not make things. Therefore I have not made this thought. I do not know its father or its mother. It is of old time before me, and therefore it is true. Man does not make truth. Man, if he be not blind, only recognizes truth when he sees it. Is this thought that I have thought a dream?"

"Perhaps it is you that are a dream," I laughed. "And that I, and sky, and sea, and the iron-hard land, are dreams, all dreams."

"I have often thought that," he assured me soberly. "It may well be so. Last night I dreamed I was a lark bird, a beautiful singing lark of the sky like the larks on the upland pastures of Haleakala. And I flew up, up, toward the sun, singing, singing, as old Kohokumu never sang. I tell you now that I dreamed I was a lark bird singing in the sky. But may not I, the real I, be the lark bird? And may not the telling of it be the dream that I, the lark bird, am dreaming now? Who are you to tell me ay or no? Dare you tell me I am not a lark bird asleep and dreaming that I am old Kohokumu?"

I shrugged my shoulders, and he continued triumphantly:

"And how do you know but what you are old Maui himself asleep and dreaming that you are John Lakana talking with me in a canoe? And may you not awake old Maui yourself, and scratch your sides and say that you had a funny dream in which you dreamed you were a haole?"

"I don't know," I admitted. "Besides, you wouldn't believe me."

"There is much more in dreams than we know," he assured me with great solemnity. "Dreams go deep, all the way down, maybe to before the beginning. May not old Maui have only dreamed he pulled Hawaii up from the bottom of the sea? Then would this Hawaii land be a dream, and you, and I, and the squid there, only parts of Maui's dream? And the lark bird too?"

He sighed and let his head sink on his breast.

"And I worry my old head about the secrets undiscoverable," he resumed, "until I grow tired and want to forget, and so I drink swipes, and go fishing, and sing old songs, and dream I am a lark bird singing in the sky. I like that best of all, and often I dream it when I have drunk much swipes . . . "

In great dejection of mood he peered down into the lagoon through the water-glass.

"There will be no more bites for a while," he announced. "The fish-sharks are prowling around, and we shall have to wait until they are gone. And so that the time shall not be heavy, I will sing you the canoe-hauling song to Lono. You remember:

"Give to me the trunk of the tree, O Lono! Give me the tree's main root, O Lono! Give me the ear of the tree, O Lono!--"

"For the love of mercy, don't sing!" I cut him short. "I've got a headache, and your singing hurts. You may be in devilish fine form to-day, but your throat is rotten. I'd rather you talked about dreams, or told me whoppers."

"It is too bad that you are sick, and you so young," he conceded cheerily. "And I shall not sing any more. I shall tell you something you do not know and have never heard; something that is no dream and no whopper, but is what I know to have happened. Not very long ago there lived here, on the beach beside this very lagoon, a young boy whose name was Keikiwai, which, as you know, means Water Baby. He was truly a water baby. His gods were the sea and fish gods, and he was born with knowledge of the language of fishes, which the fishes did not know until the sharks found it out one day when they heard him talk it.

"It happened this way. The word had been brought, and the commands, by swift runners, that the king was making a progress around the island, and that on the next day a luau" (feast) "was to be served him by the dwellers here of Waihee. It was always a hardship, when the king made a progress, for the few dwellers in small places to fill his many stomachs with food. For he came always with his wife and her women, with his priests and sorcerers, his dancers and flute-players, and hula-singers, and fighting men and servants, and his high chiefs with their wives, and sorcerers, and fighting men, and servants.

"Sometimes, in small places like Waihee, the path of his journey was marked afterward by leanness and famine. But a king must be fed, and it is not good to anger a king. So, like warning in advance of disaster, Waihee heard of his coming, and all food- getters of field and pond and mountain and sea were busied with getting food for the feast. And behold, everything was got, from the choicest of royal taro to sugar-cane joints for the roasting, from opihis to limu, from fowl to wild pig and poi-fed puppies-- everything save one thing. The fishermen failed to get lobsters.

"Now be it known that the king's favourite food was lobster. He esteemed it above all kai-kai" (food), "and his runners had made special mention of it. And there were no lobsters, and it is not good to anger a king in the belly of him. Too many sharks had come inside the reef. That was the trouble. A young girl and an old man had been eaten by them. And of the young men who dared dive for lobsters, one was eaten, and one lost an arm, and another lost one hand and one foot.

"But there was Keikiwai, the Water Baby, only eleven years old, but half fish himself and talking the language of fishes. To his father the head men came, begging him to send the Water Baby to get lobsters to fill the king's belly and divert his anger.

"Now this what happened was known and observed. For the fishermen, and their women, and the taro-growers and the bird-catchers, and the head men, and all Waihee, came down and stood back from the edge of the rock where the Water Baby stood and looked down at the lobsters far beneath on the bottom.

"And a shark, looking up with its cat's eyes, observed him, and sent out the shark-call of 'fresh meat' to assemble all the sharks in the lagoon. For the sharks work thus together, which is why they are strong. And the sharks answered the call till there were forty of them, long ones and short ones and lean ones and round ones, forty of them by count; and they talked to one another, saying: 'Look at that titbit of a child, that morsel delicious of human-flesh sweetness without the salt of the sea in it, of which salt we have too much, savoury and good to eat, melting to delight under our hearts as our bellies embrace it and extract from it its sweet.'

"Much more they said, saying: 'He has come for the lobsters. When he dives in he is for one of us. Not like the old man we ate yesterday, tough to dryness with age, nor like the young men whose members were too hard-muscled, but tender, so tender that he will melt in our gullets ere our bellies receive him. When he dives in, we will all rush for him, and the lucky one of us will get him, and, gulp, he will be gone, one bite and one swallow, into the belly of the luckiest one of us.'

"And Keikiwai, the Water Baby, heard the conspiracy, knowing the shark language; and he addressed a prayer, in the shark language, to the shark god Moku-halii, and the sharks heard and waved their tails to one another and winked their cat's eyes in token that they understood his talk. And then he said: 'I shall now dive for a lobster for the king. And no hurt shall befall me, because the shark with the shortest tail is my friend and will protect me.

"And, so saying, he picked up a chunk of lava-rock and tossed it into the water, with a big splash, twenty feet to one side. The forty sharks rushed for the splash, while he dived, and by the time they discovered they had missed him, he had gone to bottom and come back and climbed out, within his hand a fat lobster, a wahine lobster, full of eggs, for the king.

"'Ha!' said the sharks, very angry. 'There is among us a traitor. The titbit of a child, the morsel of sweetness, has spoken, and has exposed the one among us who has saved him. Let us now measure the lengths of our tails!

"Which they did, in a long row, side by side, the shorter-tailed ones cheating and stretching to gain length on themselves, the longer-tailed ones cheating and stretching in order not to be out- cheated and out-stretched. They were very angry with the one with the shortest tail, and him they rushed upon from every side and devoured till nothing was left of him.

"Again they listened while they waited for the Water Baby to dive in. And again the Water Baby made his prayer in the shark language to Moku-halii, and said: 'The shark with the shortest tail is my friend and will protect me.' And again the Water Baby tossed in a chunk of lava, this time twenty feet away off to the other side. The sharks rushed for the splash, and in their haste ran into one another, and splashed with their tails till the water was all foam, and they could see nothing, each thinking some other was swallowing the titbit. And the Water Baby came up and climbed out with another fat lobster for the king.

"And the thirty-nine sharks measured tails, devoting the one with the shortest tail, so that there were only thirty-eight sharks. And the Water Baby continued to do what I have said, and the sharks to do what I have told you, while for each shark that was eaten by his brothers there was another fat lobster laid on the rock for the king. Of course, there was much quarrelling and argument among the sharks when it came to measuring tails; but in the end it worked out in rightness and justice, for, when only two sharks were left, they were the two biggest of the original forty.

"And the Water Baby again claimed the shark with the shortest tail was his friend, fooled the two sharks with another lava-chunk, and brought up another lobster. The two sharks each claimed the other had the shorter tail, and each fought to eat the other, and the one with the longer tail won--"

"Hold, O Kohokumu!" I interrupted. "Remember that that shark had already--"

"I know just what you are going to say," he snatched his recital back from me. "And you are right. It took him so long to eat the thirty-ninth shark, for inside the thirty-ninth shark were already the nineteen other sharks he had eaten, and inside the fortieth shark were already the nineteen other sharks he had eaten, and he did not have the appetite he had started with. But do not forget he was a very big shark to begin with.

"It took him so long to eat the other shark, and the nineteen sharks inside the other shark, that he was still eating when darkness fell, and the people of Waihee went away home with all the lobsters for the king. And didn't they find the last shark on the beach next morning dead, and burst wide open with all he had eaten?"

Kohokumu fetched a full stop and held my eyes with his own shrewd ones.

"Hold, O Lakana!" he checked the speech that rushed to my tongue. "I know what next you would say. You would say that with my own eyes I did not see this, and therefore that I do not know what I have been telling you. But I do know, and I can prove it. My father's father knew the grandson of the Water Baby's father's uncle. Also, there, on the rocky point to which I point my finger now, is where the Water Baby stood and dived. I have dived for lobsters there myself. It is a great place for lobsters. Also, and often, have I seen sharks there. And there, on the bottom, as I should know, for I have seen and counted them, are the thirty- nine lava-rocks thrown in by the Water Baby as I have described."

"But--" I began.

"Ha!" he baffled me. "Look! While we have talked the fish have begun again to bite."

He pointed to three of the bamboo poles erect and devil-dancing in token that fish were hooked and struggling on the lines beneath. As he bent to his paddle, he muttered, for my benefit:

"Of course I know. The thirty-nine lava rocks are still there. You can count them any day for yourself. Of course I know, and I know for a fact."

GLEN ELLEN. October 2, 1916.

The Tears of Ah Kim

There was a great noise and racket, but no scandal, in Honolulu's Chinatown. Those within hearing distance merely shrugged their shoulders and smiled tolerantly at the disturbance as an affair of accustomed usualness. "What is it?" asked Chin Mo, down with a sharp pleurisy, of his wife, who had paused for a second at the open window to listen.

"Only Ah Kim," was her reply. "His mother is beating him again."

The fracas was taking place in the garden, behind the living rooms that were at the back of the store that fronted on the street with the proud sign above: AH KIM COMPANY, GENERAL MERCHANDISE. The garden was a miniature domain, twenty feet square, that somehow cunningly seduced the eye into a sense and seeming of illimitable vastness. There were forests of dwarf pines and oaks, centuries old yet two or three feet in height, and imported at enormous care and expense. A tiny bridge, a pace across, arched over a miniature river that flowed with rapids and cataracts from a miniature lake stocked with myriad-finned, orange-miracled goldfish that in proportion to the lake and landscape were whales. On every side the many windows of the several-storied shack-buildings looked down. In the centre of the garden, on the narrow gravelled walk close beside the lake Ah Kim was noisily receiving his beating.

No Chinese lad of tender and beatable years was Ah Kim. His was the store of Ah Kim Company, and his was the achievement of building it up through the long years from the shoestring of savings of a contract coolie labourer to a bank account in four figures and a credit that was gilt edged. An even half-century of summers and winters had passed over his head, and, in the passing, fattened him comfortably and snugly. Short of stature, his full front was as rotund as a water-melon seed. His face was moon-faced. His garb was dignified and silken, and his black-silk skull-cap with the red button atop, now, alas! fallen on the ground, was the skull-cap worn by the successful and dignified merchants of his race.

But his appearance, in this moment of the present, was anything but dignified. Dodging and ducking under a rain of blows from a bamboo cane, he was crouched over in a half-doubled posture. When he was rapped on the knuckles and elbows, with which he shielded his face and head, his winces were genuine and involuntary. From the many surrounding windows the neighbourhood looked down with placid enjoyment.

And she who wielded the stick so shrewdly from long practice! Seventy-four years old, she looked every minute of her time. Her thin legs were encased in straight-lined pants of linen stiff-textured and shiny-black. Her scraggly grey hair was drawn unrelentingly and flatly back from a narrow, unrelenting forehead. Eyebrows she had none, having long since shed them. Her eyes, of pin-hole tininess, were blackest black. She was shockingly cadaverous. Her shrivelled forearm, exposed by the loose sleeve, possessed no more of muscle than several taut bowstrings stretched across meagre bone under yellow, parchment-like skin. Along this mummy arm jade bracelets shot up and down and clashed with every blow.

"Ah!" she cried out, rhythmically accenting her blows in series of three to each shrill observation. "I forbade you to talk to Li Faa. To-day you stopped on the street with her. Not an hour ago. Half an hour by the clock you talked.--What is that?"

"It was the thrice-accursed telephone," Ah Kim muttered, while she suspended the stick to catch what he said. "Mrs. Chang Lucy told you. I know she did. I saw her see me. I shall have the telephone taken out. It is of the devil."

"It is a device of all the devils," Mrs. Tai Fu agreed, taking a fresh grip on the stick. "Yet shall the telephone remain. I like to talk with Mrs. Chang Lucy over the telephone."

"She has the eyes of ten thousand cats," quoth Ah Kim, ducking and receiving the stick stinging on his knuckles. "And the tongues of ten thousand toads," he supplemented ere his next duck.

"She is an impudent-faced and evil-mannered hussy," Mrs. Tai Fu accented.

"Mrs. Chang Lucy was ever that," Ah Kim murmured like the dutiful son he was.

"I speak of Li Faa," his mother corrected with stick emphasis. "She is only half Chinese, as you know. Her mother was a shameless kanaka. She wears skirts like the degraded haole women--also corsets, as I have seen for myself. Where are her children? Yet has she buried two husbands."

"The one was drowned, the other kicked by a horse," Ah Kim qualified.

"A year of her, unworthy son of a noble father, and you would gladly be going out to get drowned or be kicked by a horse."

Subdued chucklings and laughter from the window audience applauded her point.

"You buried two husbands yourself, revered mother," Ah Kim was stung to retort.

"I had the good taste not to marry a third. Besides, my two husbands died honourably in their beds. They were not kicked by horses nor drowned at sea. What business is it of our neighbours that you should inform them I have had two husbands, or ten, or none? You have made a scandal of me, before all our neighbours, and for that I shall now give you a real beating."

Ah Kim endured the staccato rain of blows, and said when his mother paused, breathless and weary:

"Always have I insisted and pleaded, honourable mother, that you beat me in the house, with the windows and doors closed tight, and not in the open street or the garden open behind the house.

"You have called this unthinkable Li Faa the Silvery Moon Blossom," Mrs. Tai Fu rejoined, quite illogically and femininely, but with utmost success in so far as she deflected her son from continuance of the thrust he had so swiftly driven home.

"Mrs. Chang Lucy told you," he charged.

"I was told over the telephone," his mother evaded. "I do not know all voices that speak to me over that contrivance of all the devils."

Strangely, Ah Kim made no effort to run away from his mother, which he could easily have done. She, on the other hand, found fresh cause for more stick blows.

"Ah! Stubborn one! Why do you not cry? Mule that shameth its ancestors! Never have I made you cry. From the time you were a little boy I have never made you cry. Answer me! Why do you not cry?"

Weak and breathless from her exertions, she dropped the stick and panted and shook as if with a nervous palsy.

"I do not know, except that it is my way," Ah Kim replied, gazing solicitously at his mother. "I shall bring you a chair now, and you will sit down and rest and feel better."

But she flung away from him with a snort and tottered agedly across the garden into the house. Meanwhile recovering his skull-cap and smoothing his disordered attire, Ah Kim rubbed his hurts and gazed after her with eyes of devotion. He even smiled, and almost might it appear that he had enjoyed the beating.

Ah Kim had been so beaten ever since he was a boy, when he lived on the high banks of the eleventh cataract of the Yangtse river. Here his father had been born and toiled all his days from young manhood as a towing coolie. When he died, Ah Kim, in his own young manhood, took up the same honourable profession. Farther back than all remembered annals of the family, had the males of it been towing coolies. At the time of Christ his direct ancestors had been doing the same thing, meeting the precisely similarly modelled junks below the white water at the foot of the canyon, bending the half-mile of rope to each junk, and, according to size, tailing on from a hundred to two hundred coolies of them and by sheer, two-legged man-power, bowed forward and down till their hands touched the ground and their faces were sometimes within a foot of it, dragging the junk up through the white water to the head of the canyon.

Apparently, down all the intervening centuries, the payment of the trade had not picked up. His father, his father's father, and himself, Ah Kim, had received the same invariable remuneration--per junk one-fourteenth of a cent, at the rate he had since learned money was valued in Hawaii. On long lucky summer days when the waters were easy, the junks many, the hours of daylight sixteen, sixteen hours of such heroic toil would earn over a cent. But in a whole year a towing coolie did not earn more than a dollar and a half. People could and did live on such an income. There were women servants who received a yearly wage of a dollar. The net-makers of Ti Wi earned between a dollar and two dollars a year. They lived on such wages, or, at least, they did not die on them. But for the towing coolies there were pickings, which were what made the profession honourable and the guild a close and hereditary corporation or labour union. One junk in five that was dragged up through the rapids or lowered down was wrecked. One junk in every ten was a total loss. The coolies of the towing guild knew the freaks and whims of the currents, and grappled, and raked, and netted a wet harvest from the river. They of the guild were looked up to by lesser coolies, for they could afford to drink brick tea and eat number four rice every day.

And Ah Kim had been contented and proud, until, one bitter spring day of driving sleet and hail, he dragged ashore a drowning Cantonese sailor. It was this wanderer, thawing out by his fire, who first named the magic name Hawaii to him. He had himself never been to that labourer's paradise, said the sailor; but many Chinese had gone there from Canton, and he had heard the talk of their letters written back. In Hawaii was never frost nor famine. The very pigs, never fed, were ever fat of the generous offal disdained by man. A Cantonese or Yangtse family could live on the waste of an Hawaii coolie. And wages! In gold dollars, ten a month, or, in trade dollars, two a month, was what the contract Chinese coolie received from the white-devil sugar kings. In a year the coolie received the prodigious sum of two hundred and forty trade dollars--more than a hundred times what a coolie, toiling ten times as hard, received on the eleventh cataract of the Yangtse. In short, all things considered, an Hawaii coolie was one hundred times better off, and, when the amount of labour was estimated, a thousand times better off. In addition was the wonderful climate.

When Ah Kim was twenty-four, despite his mother's pleadings and beatings, he resigned from the ancient and honourable guild of the eleventh cataract towing coolies, left his mother to go into a boss coolie's household as a servant for a dollar a year, and an annual dress to cost not less than thirty cents, and himself departed down the Yangtse to the great sea. Many were his adventures and severe his toils and hardships ere, as a salt-sea junk-sailor, he won to Canton. When he was twenty-six he signed five years of his life and labour away to the Hawaii sugar kings and departed, one of eight hundred contract coolies, for that far island land, on a festering steamer run by a crazy captain and drunken officers and rejected of Lloyds.

Honourable, among labourers, had Ah Kim's rating been as a towing coolie. In Hawaii, receiving a hundred times more pay, he found himself looked down upon as the lowest of the low--a plantation coolie, than which could be nothing lower. But a coolie whose ancestors had towed junks up the eleventh cataract of the Yangtse since before the birth of Christ inevitably inherits one character in large degree, namely, the character of patience. This patience was Ah Kim's. At the end of five years, his compulsory servitude over, thin as ever in body, in bank account he lacked just ten trade dollars of possessing a thousand trade dollars.

On this sum he could have gone back to the Yangtse and retired for life a really wealthy man. He would have possessed a larger sum, had he not, on occasion, conservatively played che fa and fan tan, and had he not, for a twelve-month, toiled among the centipedes and scorpions of the stifling cane-fields in the semi-dream of a continuous opium debauch. Why he had not toiled the whole five years under the spell of opium was the expensiveness of the habit. He had had no moral scruples. The drug had cost too much.

But Ah Kim did not return to China. He had observed the business life of Hawaii and developed a vaulting ambition. For six months, in order to learn business and English at the bottom, he clerked in the plantation store. At the end of this time he knew more about that particular store than did ever plantation manager know about any plantation store. When he resigned his position he was receiving forty gold a month, or eighty trade, and he was beginning to put on flesh. Also, his attitude toward mere contract coolies had become distinctively aristocratic. The manager offered to raise him to sixty fold, which, by the year, would constitute a fabulous fourteen hundred and forty trade, or seven hundred times his annual earning on the Yangtse as a two-legged horse at one-fourteenth of a gold cent per junk.

Instead of accepting, Ah Kim departed to Honolulu, and in the big general merchandise store of Fong & Chow Fong began at the bottom for fifteen gold per month. He worked a year and a half, and resigned when he was thirty-three, despite the seventy-five gold per month his Chinese employers were paying him. Then it was that he put up his own sign: AH KIM COMPANY, GENERAL MERCHANDISE. Also, better fed, there was about his less meagre figure a foreshadowing of the melon-seed rotundity that was to attach to him in future years.

With the years he prospered increasingly, so that, when he was thirty-six, the promise of his figure was fulfilling rapidly, and, himself a member of the exclusive and powerful Hai Gum Tong, and of the Chinese Merchants' Association, he was accustomed to sitting as host at dinners that cost him as much as thirty years of towing on the eleventh cataract would have earned him. Two things he missed: a wife, and his mother to lay the stick on him as of yore.

When he was thirty-seven he consulted his bank balance. It stood him three thousand gold. For twenty-five hundred down and an easy mortgage he could buy the three-story shack-building, and the ground in fee simple on which it stood. But to do this, left only five hundred for a wife. Fu Yee Po had a marriageable, properly small-footed daughter whom he was willing to import from China, and sell to him for eight hundred gold, plus the costs of importation. Further, Fu Yee Po was even willing to take five hundred down and the remainder on note at 6 per cent.

Ah Kim, thirty-seven years of age, fat and a bachelor, really did want a wife, especially a small-footed wife; for, China born and reared, the immemorial small-footed female had been deeply impressed into his fantasy of woman. But more, even more and far more than a small-footed wife, did he want his mother and his mother's delectable beatings. So he declined Fu Yee Po's easy terms, and at much less cost imported his own mother from servant in a boss coolie's house at a yearly wage of a dollar and a thirty-cent dress to be mistress of his Honolulu three-story shack building with two household servants, three clerks, and a porter of all work under her, to say nothing of ten thousand dollars' worth of dress goods on the shelves that ranged from the cheapest cotton crepes to the most expensive hand-embroidered silks. For be it known that even in that early day Ah Kim's emporium was beginning to cater to the tourist trade from the States.

For thirteen years Ah Kim had lived tolerably happily with his mother, and by her been methodically beaten for causes just or unjust, real or fancied; and at the end of it all he knew as strongly as ever the ache of his heart and head for a wife, and of his loins for sons to live after him, and carry on the dynasty of Ah Kim Company. Such the dream that has ever vexed men, from those early ones who first usurped a hunting right, monopolized a sandbar for a fish-trap, or stormed a village and put the males thereof to the sword. Kings, millionaires, and Chinese merchants of Honolulu have this in common, despite that they may praise God for having made them differently and in self-likable images.

And the ideal of woman that Ah Kim at fifty ached for had changed from his ideal at thirty-seven. No small-footed wife did he want now, but a free, natural, out-stepping normal-footed woman that, somehow, appeared to him in his day dreams and haunted his night visions in the form of Li Faa, the Silvery Moon Blossom. What if she were twice widowed, the daughter of a kanaka mother, the wearer of white-devil skirts and corsets and high-heeled slippers! He wanted her. It seemed it was written that she should be joint ancestor with him of the line that would continue the ownership and management through the generations, of Ah Kim Company, General Merchandise.

"I will have no half-pake daughter-in-law," his mother often reiterated to Ah Kim, pake being the Hawaiian word for Chinese. "All pake must my daughter-in-law be, even as you, my son, and as I, your mother. And she must wear trousers, my son, as all the women of our family before her. No woman, in she-devil skirts and corsets, can pay due reverence to our ancestors. Corsets and reverence do not go together. Such a one is this shameless Li Faa. She is impudent and independent, and will be neither obedient to her husband nor her husband's mother. This brazen-faced Li Faa would believe herself the source of life and the first ancestor, recognizing no ancestors before her. She laughs at our joss- sticks, and paper prayers, and family gods, as I have been well told--"

"Mrs. Chang Lucy," Ah Kim groaned.

"Not alone Mrs. Chang Lucy, O son. I have inquired. At least a dozen have heard her say of our joss house that it is all monkey foolishness. The words are hers--she, who eats raw fish, raw squid, and baked dog. Ours is the foolishness of monkeys. Yet would she marry you, a monkey, because of your store that is a palace and of the wealth that makes you a great man. And she would put shame on me, and on your father before you long honourably dead."

And there was no discussing the matter. As things were, Ah Kim knew his mother was right. Not for nothing had Li Faa been born forty years before of a Chinese father, renegade to all tradition, and of a kanaka mother whose immediate forebears had broken the taboos, cast down their own Polynesian gods, and weak-heartedly listened to the preaching about the remote and unimageable god of the Christian missionaries. Li Faa, educated, who could read and write English and Hawaiian and a fair measure of Chinese, claimed to believe in nothing, although in her secret heart she feared the kahunas (Hawaiian witch-doctors), who she was certain could charm away ill luck or pray one to death. Li Faa would never come into Ah Kim's house, as he thoroughly knew, and kow-tow to his mother and be slave to her in the immemorial Chinese way. Li Faa, from the Chinese angle, was a new woman, a feminist, who rode horseback astride, disported immodestly garbed at Waikiki on the surf-boards, and at more than one luau (feast) had been known to dance the hula with the worst and in excess of the worst, to the scandalous delight of all.

Ah Kim himself, a generation younger than his mother, had been bitten by the acid of modernity. The old order held, in so far as he still felt in his subtlest crypts of being the dusty hand of the past resting on him, residing in him; yet he subscribed to heavy policies of fire and life insurance, acted as treasurer for the local Chinese revolutionises that were for turning the Celestial Empire into a republic, contributed to the funds of the Hawaii-born Chinese baseball nine that excelled the Yankee nines at their own game, talked theosophy with Katso Suguri, the Japanese Buddhist and silk importer, fell for police graft, played and paid his insidious share in the democratic politics of annexed Hawaii, and was thinking of buying an automobile. Ah Kim never dared bare himself to himself and thrash out and winnow out how much of the old he had ceased to believe in. His mother was of the old, yet he revered her and was happy under her bamboo stick. Li Faa, the Silvery Moon Blossom, was of the new, yet he could never be quite completely happy without her.

For he loved Li Faa. Moon-faced, rotund as a water-melon seed, canny business man, wise with half a century of living-- nevertheless Ah Kim became an artist when he thought of her. He thought of her in poems of names, as woman transmuted into flower- terms of beauty and philosophic abstractions of achievement and easement. She was, to him, and alone to him of all men in the world, his Plum Blossom, his Tranquillity of Woman, his Flower of Serenity, his Moon Lily, and his Perfect Rest. And as he murmured these love endearments of namings, it seemed to him that in them were the ripplings of running waters, the tinklings of silver wind-bells, and the scents of the oleander and the jasmine. She was his poem of woman, a lyric delight, a three-dimensions of flesh and spirit delicious, a fate and a good fortune written, ere the first man and woman were, by the gods whose whim had been to make all men and women for sorrow and for joy.

But his mother put into his hand the ink-brush and placed under it, on the table, the writing tablet.

"Paint," said she, "the ideograph of TO MARRY."

He obeyed, scarcely wondering, with the deft artistry of his race and training painting the symbolic hieroglyphic.

"Resolve it," commanded his mother.

Ah Kim looked at her, curious, willing to please, unaware of the drift of her intent.

"Of what is it composed?" she persisted. "What are the three originals, the sum of which is it: to marry, marriage, the coming together and wedding of a man and a woman? Paint them, paint them apart, the three originals, unrelated, so that we may know how the wise men of old wisely built up the ideograph of to marry."

And Ah Kim, obeying and painting, saw that what he had painted were three picture-signs--the picture-signs of a hand, an ear, and a woman.

"Name them," said his mother; and he named them.

"It is true," said she. "It is a great tale. It is the stuff of the painted pictures of marriage. Such marriage was in the beginning; such shall it always be in my house. The hand of the man takes the woman's ear, and by it leads her away to his house, where she is to be obedient to him and to his mother. I was taken by the ear, so, by your long honourably dead father. I have looked at your hand. It is not like his hand. Also have I looked at the ear of Li Faa. Never will you lead her by the ear. She has not that kind of an ear. I shall live a long time yet, and I will be mistress in my son's house, after our ancient way, until I die."

"But she is my revered ancestress," Ah Kim explained to Li Faa.

He was timidly unhappy; for Li Faa, having ascertained that Mrs. Tai Fu was at the temple of the Chinese AEsculapius making a food offering of dried duck and prayers for her declining health, had taken advantage of the opportunity to call upon him in his store.

Li Faa pursed her insolent, unpainted lips into the form of a half-opened rosebud, and replied:

"That will do for China. I do not know China. This is Hawaii, and in Hawaii the customs of all foreigners change."

"She is nevertheless my ancestress," Ah Kim protested, "the mother who gave me birth, whether I am in China or Hawaii, O Silvery Moon Blossom that I want for wife."

"I have had two husbands," Li Faa stated placidly. "One was a pake, one was a Portuguese. I learned much from both. Also am I educated. I have been to High School, and I have played the piano in public. And I learned from my two husbands much. The pake makes the best husband. Never again will I marry anything but a pake. But he must not take me by the ear--"

"How do you know of that?" he broke in suspiciously.

"Mrs. Chang Lucy," was the reply. "Mrs. Chang Lucy tells me everything that your mother tells her, and your mother tells her much. So let me tell you that mine is not that kind of an ear."

"Which is what my honoured mother has told me," Ah Kim groaned.

"Which is what your honoured mother told Mrs. Chang Lucy, which is what Mrs. Chang Lucy told me," Li Faa completed equably. "And I now tell you, O Third Husband To Be, that the man is not born who will lead me by the ear. It is not the way in Hawaii. I will go only hand in hand with my man, side by side, fifty-fifty as is the haole slang just now. My Portuguese husband thought different. He tried to beat me. I landed him three times in the police court and each time he worked out his sentence on the reef. After that he got drowned."

"My mother has been my mother for fifty years," Ah Kim declared stoutly.

"And for fifty years has she beaten you," Li Faa giggled. "How my father used to laugh at Yap Ten Shin! Like you, Yap Ten Shin had been born in China, and had brought the China customs with him. His old father was for ever beating him with a stick. He loved his father. But his father beat him harder than ever when he became a missionary pake. Every time he went to the missionary services, his father beat him. And every time the missionary heard of it he was harsh in his language to Yap Ten Shin for allowing his father to beat him. And my father laughed and laughed, for my father was a very liberal pake, who had changed his customs quicker than most foreigners. And all the trouble was because Yap Ten Shin had a loving heart. He loved his honourable father. He loved the God of Love of the Christian missionary. But in the end, in me, he found the greatest love of all, which is the love of woman. In me he forgot his love for his father and his love for the loving Christ.

"And he offered my father six hundred gold, for me--the price was small because my feet were not small. But I was half kanaka. I said that I was not a slave-woman, and that I would be sold to no man. My high-school teacher was a haole old maid who said love of woman was so beyond price that it must never be sold. Perhaps that is why she was an old maid. She was not beautiful. She could not give herself away. My kanaka mother said it was not the kanaka way to sell their daughters for a money price. They gave their daughters for love, and she would listen to reason if Yap Ten Shin provided luaus in quantity and quality. My pake father, as I have told you, was liberal. He asked me if I wanted Yap Ten Shin for my husband. And I said yes; and freely, of myself, I went to him. He it was who was kicked by a horse; but he was a very good husband before he was kicked by the horse.

"As for you, Ah Kim, you shall always be honourable and lovable for me, and some day, when it is not necessary for you to take me by the ear, I shall marry you and come here and be with you always, and you will be the happiest pake in all Hawaii; for I have had two husbands, and gone to high school, and am most wise in making a husband happy. But that will be when your mother has ceased to beat you. Mrs. Chang Lucy tells me that she beats you very hard."

"She does," Ah Kim affirmed. "Behold! He thrust back his loose sleeves, exposing to the elbow his smooth and cherubic forearms. They were mantled with black and blue marks that advertised the weight and number of blows so shielded from his head and face.

"But she has never made me cry," Ah Kim disclaimed hastily. "Never, from the time I was a little boy, has she made me cry."

"So Mrs. Chang Lucy says," Li Faa observed. "She says that your honourable mother often complains to her that she has never made you cry."

A sibilant warning from one of his clerks was too late. Having regained the house by way of the back alley, Mrs. Tai Fu emerged right upon them from out of the living apartments. Never had Ah Kim seen his mother's eyes so blazing furious. She ignored Li Faa, as she screamed at him:

"Now will I make you cry. As never before shall I beat you until you do cry."

"Then let us go into the back rooms, honourable mother," Ah Kim suggested. "We will close the windows and the doors, and there may you beat me."

"No. Here shall you be beaten before all the world and this shameless woman who would, with her own hand, take you by the ear and call such sacrilege marriage! Stay, shameless woman."

"I am going to stay anyway," said Li Faa. She favoured the clerks with a truculent stare. "And I'd like to see anything less than the police put me out of here."

"You will never be my daughter-in-law," Mrs. Tai Fu snapped.

Li Faa nodded her head in agreement.

"But just the same," she added, "shall your son be my third husband."

"You mean when I am dead?" the old mother screamed.

"The sun rises each morning," Li Faa said enigmatically. "All my life have I seen it rise--"

"You are forty, and you wear corsets."

"But I do not dye my hair--that will come later," Li Faa calmly retorted. "As to my age, you are right. I shall be forty-one next Kamehameha Day. For forty years I have seen the sun rise. My father was an old man. Before he died he told me that he had observed no difference in the rising of the sun since when he was a little boy. The world is round. Confucius did not know that, but you will find it in all the geography books. The world is round. Ever it turns over on itself, over and over and around and around. And the times and seasons of weather and life turn with it. What is, has been before. What has been, will be again. The time of the breadfruit and the mango ever recurs, and man and woman repeat themselves. The robins nest, and in the springtime the plovers come from the north. Every spring is followed by another spring. The coconut palm rises into the air, ripens its fruit, and departs. But always are there more coconut palms. This is not all my own smart talk. Much of it my father told me. Proceed, honourable Mrs. Tai Fu, and beat your son who is my Third Husband To Be. But I shall laugh. I warn you I shall laugh."

Ah Kim dropped down on his knees so as to give his mother every advantage. And while she rained blows upon him with the bamboo stick, Li Faa smiled and giggled, and finally burst into laughter.

"Harder, O honourable Mrs. Tai Fu!" Li Faa urged between paroxysms of mirth.

Mrs. Tai Fu did her best, which was notably weak, until she observed what made her drop the stick by her side in amazement. Ah Kim was crying. Down both cheeks great round tears were coursing. Li Faa was amazed. So were the gaping clerks. Most amazed of all was Ah Kim, yet he could not help himself; and, although no further blows fell, he cried steadily on.

"But why did you cry?" Li Faa demanded often of Ah Kim. "It was so perfectly foolish a thing to do. She was not even hurting you."

"Wait until we are married," was Ah Kim's invariable reply, "and then, O Moon Lily, will I tell you."

Two years later, one afternoon, more like a water-melon seed in configuration than ever, Ah Kim returned home from a meeting of the Chinese Protective Association, to find his mother dead on her couch. Narrower and more unrelenting than ever were the forehead and the brushed-back hair. But on her face was a withered smile. The gods had been kind. She had passed without pain.

He telephoned first of all to Li Faa's number but did not find her until he called up Mrs. Chang Lucy. The news given, the marriage was dated ahead with ten times the brevity of the old-line Chinese custom. And if there be anything analogous to a bridesmaid in a Chinese wedding, Mrs. Chang Lucy was just that.

"Why," Li Faa asked Ah Kim when alone with him on their wedding night, "why did you cry when your mother beat you that day in the store? You were so foolish. She was not even hurting you."

"That is why I cried," answered Ah Kim.

Li Faa looked up at him without understanding.

"I cried," he explained, "because I suddenly knew that my mother was nearing her end. There was no weight, no hurt, in her blows. I cried because I knew SHE NO LONGER HAD STRENGTH ENOUGH TO HURT ME. That is why I cried, my Flower of Serenity, my Perfect Rest. That is the only reason why I cried."

WAIKIKI, HONOLULU. June 16, 1916.

The Kanaka Surf

The tourist women, under the hau tree arbour that lines the Moana hotel beach, gasped when Lee Barton and his wife Ida emerged from the bath-house. And as the pair walked past them and down to the sand, they continued to gasp. Not that there was anything about Lee Barton provocative of gasps. The tourist women were not of the sort to gasp at sight of a mere man's swimming-suited body, no matter with what swelling splendour of line and muscle such body was invested. Nevertheless, trainers and conditioners of men would have drawn deep breaths of satisfaction at contemplation of the physical spectacle of him. But they would not have gasped in the way the women did, whose gasps were indicative of moral shock.

Ida Barton was the cause of their perturbation and disapproval. They disapproved, seriously so, at the first instant's glimpse of her. They thought--such ardent self-deceivers were they--that they were shocked by her swimming suit. But Freud has pointed out how persons, where sex is involved, are prone sincerely to substitute one thing for another thing, and to agonize over the substituted thing as strenuously as if it were the real thing.

Ida Barton's swimming suit was a very nice one, as women's suits go. Of thinnest of firm-woven black wool, with white trimmings and a white belt-line, it was high-throated, short-sleeved, and brief- skirted. Brief as was the skirt, the leg-tights were no less brief. Yet on the beach in front of the adjacent Outrigger Club, and entering and leaving the water, a score of women, not provoking gasping notice, were more daringly garbed. Their men's suits, as brief of leg-tights and skirts, fitted them as snugly, but were sleeveless after the way of men's suits, the arm-holes deeply low- cut and in-cut, and, by the exposed armpits, advertiseful that the wearers were accustomed to 1916 decollete.

So it was not Ida Barton's suit, although the women deceived themselves into thinking it was. It was, first of all, say her legs; or, first of all, say the totality of her, the sweet and brilliant jewel of her femininity bursting upon them. Dowager, matron, and maid, conserving their soft-fat muscles or protecting their hot-house complexions in the shade of the hau-tree arbour, felt the immediate challenge of her. She was menace as well, an affront of superiority in their own chosen and variously successful game of life.

But they did not say it. They did not permit themselves to think it. They thought it was the suit, and said so to one another, ignoring the twenty women more daringly clad but less perilously beautiful. Could one have winnowed out of the souls of these disapproving ones what lay at bottom of their condemnation of her suit, it would have been found to be the sex-jealous thought: THAT NO WOMAN, SO BEAUTIFUL AS THIS ONE, SHOULD BE PERMITTED TO SHOW HER BEAUTY. It was not fair to them. What chance had they in the conquering of males with so dangerous a rival in the foreground?

They were justified. As Stanley Patterson said to his wife, where the two of them lolled wet in the sand by the tiny fresh-water stream that the Bartons waded in order to gain the Outrigger Club beach:

"Lord god of models and marvels, behold them! My dear, did you ever see two such legs on one small woman! Look at the roundness and taperingness. They're boy's legs. I've seen featherweights go into the ring with legs like those. And they're all-woman's legs, too. Never mistake them in the world. The arc of the front line of that upper leg! And the balanced adequate fullness at the back! And the way the opposing curves slender in to the knee that IS a knee! Makes my fingers itch. Wish I had some clay right now."

"It's a true human knee," his wife concurred, no less breathlessly; for, like her husband, she was a sculptor. "Look at the joint of it working under the skin. It's got form, and blessedly is not covered by a bag of fat." She paused to sigh, thinking of her own knees. "It's correct, and beautiful, and dainty. Charm! If ever I beheld the charm of flesh, it is now. I wonder who she is."

Stanley Patterson, gazing ardently, took up his half of the chorus.

"Notice that the round muscle-pads on the inner sides that make most women appear knock-kneed are missing. They're boy's legs, firm and sure--"

"And sweet woman's legs, soft and round," his wife hastened to balance. "And look, Stanley! See how she walks on the balls of her feet. It makes her seem light as swan's down. Each step seems just a little above the earth, and each other step seems just a little higher above until you get the impression she is flying, or just about to rise and begin flying . . . "

So Stanley and Mrs. Patterson. But they were artists, with eyes therefore unlike the next batteries of human eyes Ida Barton was compelled to run, and that laired on the Outrigger lanais (verandas) and in the hau-tree shade of the closely adjoining seaside. The majority of the Outrigger audience was composed, not of tourist guests, but of club members and old-timers in Hawaii. And even the old-times women gasped.

"It's positively indecent," said Mrs. Hanley Black to her husband, herself a too-stout-in-the-middle matron of forty-five, who had been born in the Hawaiian islands, and who had never heard of Ostend.

Hanley Black surveyed his wife's criminal shapelessness and voluminousness of antediluvian, New-England swimming dress with a withering, contemplative eye. They had been married a sufficient number of years for him frankly to utter his judgment.

"That strange woman's suit makes your own look indecent. You appear as a creature shameful, under a grotesqueness of apparel striving to hide some secret awfulness."

"She carries her body like a Spanish dancer," Mrs. Patterson said to her husband, for the pair of them had waded the little stream in pursuit of the vision.

"By George, she does," Stanley Patterson concurred. "Reminds me of Estrellita. Torso just well enough forward, slender waist, not too lean in the stomach, and with muscles like some lad boxer's armouring that stomach to fearlessness. She has to have them to carry herself that way and to balance the back muscles. See that muscled curve of the back! It's Estrellita's."

"How tall would you say?" his wife queried.

"There she deceives," was the appraised answer. "She might be five-feet-one, or five-feet-three or four. It's that way she has of walking that you described as almost about to fly."

"Yes, that's it," Mrs. Patterson concurred. "It's her energy, her seemingness of being on tip toe with rising vitality."

Stanley Patterson considered for a space.

"That's it," he enounced. "She IS a little thing. I'll give her five-two in her stockings. And I'll weigh her a mere one hundred and ten, or eight, or fifteen at the outside."

"She won't weigh a hundred and ten," his wife declared with conviction.

"And with her clothes on, plus her carriage (which is builded of her vitality and will), I'll wager she'd never impress any one with her smallness."

"I know her type," his wife nodded. "You meet her out, and you have the sense that, while not exactly a fine large woman, she's a whole lot larger than the average. And now, age?"

"I'll give you best there," he parried.

"She might be twenty-five, she might be twenty-eight . . . "

But Stanley Patterson had impolitely forgotten to listen.

"It's not her legs alone," he cried on enthusiastically. "It's the all of her. Look at the delicacy of that forearm. And the swell of line to the shoulder. And that biceps! It's alive. Dollars to drowned kittens she can flex a respectable knot of it . . . "

No woman, much less an Ida Barton, could have been unconscious of the effect she was producing along Waikiki Beach. Instead of making her happy in the small vanity way, it irritated her.

"The cats," she laughed to her husband. "And to think I was born here an almost even third of a century ago! But they weren't nasty then. Maybe because there weren't any tourists. Why, Lee, I learned to swim right here on this beach in front of the Outrigger. We used to come out with daddy for vacations and for week-ends and sort of camp out in a grass house that stood right where the Outrigger ladies serve tea now. And centipedes fell out of the thatch on us, while we slept, and we all ate poi and opihis and raw aku, and nobody wore much of anything for the swimming and squidding, and there was no real road to town. I remember times of big rain when it was so flooded we had to go in by canoe, out through the reef and in by Honolulu Harbour."

"Remember," Lee Barton added, "it was just about that time that the youngster that became me arrived here for a few weeks' stay on our way around. I must have seen you on the beach at that very time-- one of the kiddies that swam like fishes. Why, merciful me, the women here were all riding cross-saddle, and that was long before the rest of the social female world outgrew its immodesty and came around to sitting simultaneously on both sides of a horse. I learned to swim on the beach here at that time myself. You and I may even have tried body-surfing on the same waves, or I may have splashed a handful of water into your mouth and been rewarded by your sticking out your tongue at me--"

Interrupted by an audible gasp of shock from a spinster-appearing female sunning herself hard by and angularly in the sand in a swimming suit monstrously unbeautiful, Lee Barton was aware of an involuntary and almost perceptible stiffening on the part of his wife.

"I smile with pleasure," he told her. "It serves only to make your valiant little shoulders the more valiant. It may make you self-conscious, but it likewise makes you absurdly self-confident."

For, be it known in advance, Lee Barton was a super-man and Ida Barton a super-woman--or at least they were personalities so designated by the cub book-reviewers, flat-floor men and women, and scholastically emasculated critics, who from across the dreary levels of their living can descry no glorious humans over-topping their horizons. These dreary folk, echoes of the dead past and importunate and self-elected pall-bearers for the present and future, proxy-livers of life and vicarious sensualists that they are in a eunuch sort of way, insist, since their own selves, environments, and narrow agitations of the quick are mediocre and commonplace, that no man or woman can rise above the mediocre and commonplace.

Lacking gloriousness in themselves, they deny gloriousness to all mankind; too cowardly for whimsy and derring-do, they assert whimsy and derring-do ceased at the very latest no later than the middle ages; flickering little tapers themselves, their feeble eyes are dazzled to unseeingness of the flaming conflagrations of other souls that illumine their skies. Possessing power in no greater quantity than is the just due of pygmies, they cannot conceive of power greater in others than in themselves. In those days there were giants; but, as their mouldy books tell them, the giants are long since passed, and only the bones of them remain. Never having seen the mountains, there are no mountains.

In the mud of their complacently perpetuated barnyard pond, they assert that no bright-browed, bright-apparelled shining figures can be outside of fairy books, old histories, and ancient superstitions. Never having seen the stars, they deny the stars. Never having glimpsed the shining ways nor the mortals that tread them, they deny the existence of the shinning ways as well as the existence of the high-bright mortals who adventure along the shining ways. The narrow pupils of their eyes the centre of the universe, they image the universe in terms of themselves, of their meagre personalities make pitiful yardsticks with which to measure the high-bright souls, saying: "Thus long are all souls, and no longer; it is impossible that there should exist greater-statured souls than we are, and our gods know that we are great of stature."

But all, or nearly all on the beach, forgave Ida Barton her suit and form when she took the water. A touch of her hand on her husband's arm, indication and challenge in her laughing face, and the two ran as one for half a dozen paces and leapt as one from the hard-wet sand of the beach, their bodies describing flat arches of flight ere the water was entered.

There are two surfs at Waikiki: the big, bearded man surf that roars far out beyond the diving-stage; the smaller, gentler, wahine, or woman, surf that breaks upon the shore itself. Here is a great shallowness, where one may wade a hundred or several hundred feet to get beyond depth. Yet, with a good surf on outside, the wahine surf can break three or four feet, so that, close in against the shore, the hard-sand bottom may be three feet or three inches under the welter of surface foam. To dive from the beach into this, to fly into the air off racing feet, turn in mid- flight so that heels are up and head is down, and, so to enter the water head-first, requires wisdom of waves, timing of waves, and a trained deftness in entering such unstable depths of water with pretty, unapprehensive, head-first cleavage, while at the same time making the shallowest possible of dives.

It is a sweet, and pretty, and daring trick, not learned in a day, nor learned at all without many a milder bump on the bottom or close shave of fractured skull or broken neck. Here, on the spot where the Bartons so beautifully dived, two days before a Stanford track athlete had broken his neck. His had been an error in timing the rise and subsidence of a wahine wave.

"A professional," Mrs. Hanley Black sneered to her husband at Ida Barton's feat.

"Some vaudeville tank girl," was one of the similar remarks with which the women in the shade complacently reassured one another-- finding, by way of the weird mental processes of self-illusion, a great satisfaction in the money caste-distinction between one who worked for what she ate and themselves who did not work for what they ate.

It was a day of heavy surf on Waikiki. In the wahine surf it was boisterous enough for good swimmers. But out beyond, in the kanaka, or man, surf, no one ventured. Not that the score or more of young surf-riders loafing on the beach could not venture there, or were afraid to venture there; but because their biggest outrigger canoes would have been swamped, and their surf-boards would have been overwhelmed in the too-immense over-topple and down-fall of the thundering monsters. They themselves, most of them, could have swum, for man can swim through breakers which canoes and surf-boards cannot surmount; but to ride the backs of the waves, rise out of the foam to stand full length in the air above, and with heels winged with the swiftness of horses to fly shoreward, was what made sport for them and brought them out from Honolulu to Waikiki.

The captain of Number Nine canoe, himself a charter member of the Outrigger and a many-times medallist in long-distance swimming, had missed seeing the Bartons take the water, and first glimpsed them beyond the last festoon of bathers clinging to the life-lines. From then on, from his vantage of the upstairs lanai, he kept his eyes on them. When they continued out past the steel diving-stage where a few of the hardiest divers disported, he muttered vexedly under his breath "damned malahinis!"

Now malahini means new-comer, tender-foot; and, despite the prettiness of their stroke, he knew that none except malahinis would venture into the racing channel beyond the diving-stage. Hence the vexation of the captain of Number Nine. He descended to the beach, with a low word here and there picked a crew of the strongest surfers, and returned to the lanai with a pair of binoculars. Quite casually, the crew, six of them, carried Number Nine to the water's edge, saw paddles and everything in order for a quick launching, and lolled about carelessly on the sand. They were guilty of not advertising that anything untoward was afoot, although they did steal glances up to their captain straining through the binoculars.

What made the channel was the fresh-water stream. Coral cannot abide fresh water. What made the channel race was the immense shoreward surf-fling of the sea. Unable to remain flung up on the beach, pounded ever back toward the beach by the perpetual shoreward rush of the kanaka surf, the up-piled water escaped to the sea by way of the channel and in the form of under-tow along the bottom under the breakers. Even in the channel the waves broke big, but not with the magnificent bigness of terror as to right and left. So it was that a canoe or a comparatively strong swimmer could dare the channel. But the swimmer must be a strong swimmer indeed, who could successfully buck the current in. Wherefore the captain of Number Nine continued his vigil and his muttered damnation of malahinis, disgustedly sure that these two malahinis would compel him to launch Number Nine and go after them when they found the current too strong to swim in against. As for himself, caught in their predicament, he would have veered to the left toward Diamond Head and come in on the shoreward fling of the kanaka surf. But then, he was no one other than himself, a bronze. Hercules of twenty-two, the whitest blond man ever burned to mahogany brown by a sub-tropic sun, with body and lines and muscles very much resembling the wonderful ones of Duke Kahanamoku. In a hundred yards the world champion could invariably beat him a second flat; but over a distance of miles he could swim circles around the champion.

No one of the many hundreds on the beach, with the exception of till captain and his crew, knew that the Bartons had passed beyond the diving-stage. All who had watched them start to swim out had taken for granted that they had joined the others on the stage.

The captain suddenly sprang upon the railing of the lanai, held on to a pillar with one hand, and again picked up the two specks of heads through the glasses. His surprise was verified. The two fools had veered out of the channel toward Diamond Head, and were directly seaward of the kanaka surf. Worse, as he looked, they were starting to come in through the kanaka surf.

He glanced down quickly to the canoe, and even as he glanced, and as the apparently loafing members quietly arose and took their places by the canoe for the launching, he achieved judgment. Before the canoe could get abreast in the channel, all would be over with the man and woman. And, granted that it could get abreast of them, the moment it ventured into the kanaka surf it would be swamped, and a sorry chance would the strongest swimmer of them have of rescuing a person pounding to pulp on the bottom under the smashes of the great bearded ones.

The captain saw the first kanaka wave, large of itself, but small among its fellows, lift seaward behind the two speck-swimmers. Then he saw them strike a crawl-stroke, side by side, faces downward, full-lengths out-stretched on surface, their feet sculling like propellers and their arms flailing in rapid over-hand strokes, as they spurted speed to approximate the speed of the overtaking wave, so that, when overtaken, they would become part of the wave, and travel with it instead of being left behind it. Thus, if they were coolly skilled enough to ride outstretched on the surface and the forward face of the crest instead of being flung and crumpled or driven head-first to bottom, they would dash shoreward, not propelled by their own energy, but by the energy of the wave into which they had become incorporated.

And they did it! "SOME swimmers!" the captain of Number Nine made announcement to himself under his breath. He continued to gaze eagerly. The best of swimmers could hold such a wave for several hundred feet. But could they? If they did, they would be a third of the way through the perils they had challenged. But, not unexpected by him, the woman failed first, her body not presenting the larger surfaces that her husband's did. At the end of seventy feet she was overwhelmed, being driven downward and out of sight by the tons of water in the over-topple. Her husband followed and both appeared swimming beyond the wave they had lost.

The captain saw the next wave first. "If they try to body-surf on that, good night," he muttered; for he knew the swimmer did not live who would tackle it. Beardless itself, it was father of all bearded ones, a mile long, rising up far out beyond where the others rose, towering its solid bulk higher and higher till it blotted out the horizon, and was a giant among its fellows ere its beard began to grow as it thinned its crest to the over-curl.

But it was evident that the man and woman knew big water. No racing stroke did they make in advance of the wave. The captain inwardly applauded as he saw them turn and face the wave and wait for it. It was a picture that of all on the beach he alone saw, wonderfully distinct and vivid in the magnification of the binoculars. The wall of the wave was truly a wall, mounting, ever mounting, and thinning, far up, to a transparency of the colours of the setting sun shooting athwart all the green and blue of it. The green thinned to lighter green that merged blue even as he looked. But it was a blue gem-brilliant with innumerable sparkle-points of rose and gold flashed through it by the sun. On and up, to the sprouting beard of growing crest, the colour orgy increased until it was a kaleidoscopic effervescence of transfusing rainbows.

Against the face of the wave showed the heads of the man and woman like two sheer specks. Specks they were, of the quick, adventuring among the blind elemental forces, daring the titanic buffets of the sea. The weight of the down-fall of that father of waves, even then imminent above their heads, could stun a man or break the fragile bones of a woman. The captain of Number Nine was unconscious that he was holding his breath. He was oblivious of the man. It was the woman. Did she lose her head or courage, or misplay her muscular part for a moment, she could be hurled a hundred feet by that giant buffet and left wrenched, helpless, and breathless to be pulped on the coral bottom and sucked out by the undertow to be battened on by the fish-sharks too cowardly to take their human meat alive.

Why didn't they dive deep, and with plenty of time, the captain wanted to know, instead of waiting till the last tick of safety and the first tick of peril were one? He saw the woman turn her head and laugh to the man, and his head turn in response. Above them, overhanging them, as they mounted the body of the wave, the beard, creaming white, then frothing into rose and gold, tossed upward into a spray of jewels. The crisp off-shore trade-wind caught the beard's fringes and blew them backward and upward yards and yards into the air. It was then, side by side, and six feet apart, that they dived straight under the over-curl even then disintegrating to chaos and falling. Like insects disappearing into the convolutions of some gorgeous gigantic orchid, so they disappeared, as beard and crest and spray and jewels, in many tons, crashed and thundered down just where they had disappeared the moment before, but where they were no longer.

Beyond the wave they had gone through, they finally showed, side by side, still six feet apart, swimming shoreward with a steady stroke until the next wave should make them body-surf it or face and pierce it. The captain of Number Nine waved his hand to his crew in dismissal, and sat down on the lanai railing, feeling vaguely tired and still watching the swimmers through his glasses.

"Whoever and whatever they are," he murmured, "they aren't malahinis. They simply can't be malahinis."

Not all days, and only on rare days, is the surf heavy at Waikiki; and, in the days that followed, Ida and Lee Barton, much in evidence on the beach and in the water, continued to arouse disparaging interest in the breasts of the tourist ladies, although the Outrigger captains ceased from worrying about them in the water. They would watch the pair swim out and disappear in the blue distance, and they might, or might not, chance to see them return hours afterward. The point was that the captains did not bother about their returning, because they knew they would return.

The reason for this was that they were not malahinis. They belonged. In other words, or, rather, in the potent Islands-word, they were kamaaina. Kamaaina men and women of forty remembered Lee Barton from their childhood days, when, in truth, he had been a malahini, though a very young specimen. Since that time, in the course of various long stays, he had earned the kamaaina distinction.

As for Ida Barton, young matrons of her own age (privily wondering how she managed to keep her figure) met her with arms around and hearty Hawaiian kisses. Grandmothers must have her to tea and reminiscence in old gardens of forgotten houses which the tourist never sees. Less than a week after her arrival, the aged Queen Liliuokalani must send for her and chide her for neglect. And old men, on cool and balmy lanais, toothlessly maundered to her about Grandpa Captain Wilton, of before their time, but whose wild and lusty deeds and pranks, told them by their fathers, they remembered with gusto--Grandpa Captain Wilton, or David Wilton, or "All Hands" as the Hawaiians of that remote day had affectionately renamed him. All Hands, ex-Northwest trader, the godless, beach-combing, clipper-shipless and ship-wrecked skipper who had stood on the beach at Kailua and welcomed the very first of missionaries, off the brig Thaddeus, in the year 1820, and who, not many years later, made a scandalous runaway marriage with one of their daughters, quieted down and served the Kamehamehas long and conservatively as Minister of the Treasury and Chief of the Customs, and acted as intercessor and mediator between the missionaries on one side and the beach-combing crowd, the trading crowd, and the Hawaiian chiefs on the variously shifting other side.

Nor was Lee Barton neglected. In the midst of the dinners and lunches, the luaus (Hawaiian feasts) and poi-suppers, and swims and dances in aloha (love) to both of them, his time and inclination were claimed by the crowd of lively youngsters of old Kohala days who had come to know that they possessed digestions and various other internal functions, and who had settled down to somewhat of sedateness, who roistered less, and who played bridge much, and went to baseball often. Also, similarly oriented, was the old poker crowd of Lee Barton's younger days, which crowd played for more consistent stakes and limits, while it drank mineral water and orange juice and timed the final round of "Jacks" never later than midnight.

Appeared, through all the rout of entertainment, Sonny Grandison, Hawaii-born, Hawaii-prominent, who, despite his youthful forty-one years, had declined the proffered governorship of the Territory. Also, he had ducked Ida Barton in the surf at Waikiki a quarter of a century before, and, still earlier, vacationing on his father's great Lakanaii cattle ranch, had hair-raisingly initiated her, and various other tender tots of five to seven years of age, into his boys' band, "The Cannibal Head-Hunters" or "The Terrors of Lakanaii." Still farther, his Grandpa Grandison and her Grandpa Wilton had been business and political comrades in the old days.

Educated at Harvard, he had become for a time a world-wandering scientist and social favourite. After serving in the Philippines, he had accompanied various expeditions through Malaysia, South America, and Africa in the post of official entomologist. At forty-one he still retained his travelling commission from the Smithsonian Institution, while his friends insisted that he knew more about sugar "bugs" than the expert entomologists employed by him and his fellow sugar planters in the Experiment Station. Bulking large at home, he was the best-known representative of Hawaii abroad. It was the axiom among travelled Hawaii folk, that wherever over the world they might mention they were from Hawaii, the invariable first question asked of them was: "And do you know Sonny Grandison?"

In brief, he was a wealthy man's son who had made good. His father's million he inherited he had increased to ten millions, at the same time keeping up his father's benefactions and endowments and overshadowing them with his own.

But there was still more to him. A ten years' widower, without issue, he was the most eligible and most pathetically sought-after marriageable man in all Hawaii. A clean-and-strong-featured brunette, tall, slenderly graceful, with the lean runner's stomach, always fit as a fiddle, a distinguished figure in any group, the greying of hair over his temples (in juxtaposition to his young- textured skin and bright vital eyes) made him appear even more distinguished. Despite the social demands upon his time, and despite his many committee meetings, and meetings of boards of directors and political conferences, he yet found time and space to captain the Lakanaii polo team to more than occasional victory, and on his own island of Lakanaii vied with the Baldwins of Maui in the breeding and importing of polo ponies.

Given a markedly strong and vital man and woman, when a second equally markedly strong and vital man enters the scene, the peril of a markedly strong and vital triangle of tragedy becomes imminent. Indeed, such a triangle of tragedy may be described, in the terminology of the flat-floor folk, as "super" and "impossible." Perhaps, since within himself originated the desire and the daring, it was Sonny Grandison who first was conscious of the situation, although he had to be quick to anticipate the sensing intuition of a woman like Ida Barton. At any rate, and undebatable, the last of the three to attain awareness was Lee Barton, who promptly laughed away what was impossible to laugh away.

His first awareness, he quickly saw, was so belated that half his hosts and hostesses were already aware. Casting back, he realized that for some time any affair to which he and his wife were invited found Sonny Grandison likewise invited. Wherever the two had been, the three had been. To Kahuku or to Haleiwa, to Ahuimanu, or to Kaneohe for the coral gardens, or to Koko Head for a picnicking and a swimming, somehow it invariably happened that Ida rode in Sonny's car or that both rode in somebody's car. Dances, luaus, dinners, and outings were all one; the three of them were there.

Having become aware, Lee Barton could not fail to register Ida's note of happiness ever rising when in the same company with Sonny Grandison, and her willingness to ride in the same cars with him, to dance with him, or to sit out dances with him. Most convincing of all, was Sonny Grandison himself. Forty-one, strong, experienced, his face could no more conceal what he felt than could be concealed a lad of twenty's ordinary lad's love. Despite the control and restraint of forty years, he could no more mask his soul with his face than could Lee Barton, of equal years, fail to read that soul through so transparent a face. And often, to other women, talking, when the topic of Sonny came up, Lee Barton heard Ida express her fondness for Sonny, or her almost too-eloquent appreciation of his polo-playing, his work in the world, and his general all-rightness of achievement.

About Sonny's state of mind and heart Lee had no doubt. It was patent enough for the world to read. But how about Ida, his own dozen-years' wife of a glorious love-match? He knew that woman, ever the mysterious sex, was capable any time of unguessed mystery. Did her frank comradeliness with Grandison token merely frank comradeliness and childhood contacts continued and recrudesced into adult years? or did it hide, in woman's subtler and more secretive ways, a beat of heart and return of feeling that might even out-balance what Sonny's face advertised?

Lee Barton was not happy. A dozen years of utmost and post-nuptial possession of his wife had proved to him, so far as he was concerned, that she was his one woman in the world, and that the woman was unborn, much less unglimpsed, who could for a moment compete with her in his heart, his soul, and his brain. Impossible of existence was the woman who could lure him away from her, much less over-bid her in the myriad, continual satisfactions she rendered him.

Was this, then, he asked himself, the dreaded contingency of all fond Benedicts, to be her first "affair?" He tormented himself with the ever iterant query, and, to the astonishment of the reformed Kohala poker crowd of wise and middle-aged youngsters as well as to the reward of the keen scrutiny of the dinner-giving and dinner-attending women, he began to drink King William instead of orange juice, to bully up the poker limit, to drive of nights his own car more than rather recklessly over the Pali and Diamond Head roads, and, ere dinner or lunch or after, to take more than an average man's due of old-fashioned cocktails and Scotch highs.

All the years of their marriage she had been ever complaisant toward him in his card-playing. This complaisance, to him, had become habitual. But now that doubt had arisen, it seemed to him that he noted an eagerness in her countenancing of his poker parties. Another point he could not avoid noting was that Sonny Grandison was missed by the poker and bridge crowds. He seemed to be too busy. Now where was Sonny, while he, Lee Barton, was playing? Surely not always at committee and boards of directors meetings. Lee Barton made sure of this. He easily learned that at such times Sonny was more than usually wherever Ida chanced to be-- at dances, or dinners, or moonlight swimming parties, or, the very afternoon he had flatly pleaded rush of affairs as an excuse not to join Lee and Langhorne Jones and Jack Holstein in a bridge battle at the Pacific Club--that afternoon he had played bridge at Dora Niles' home with three women, one of whom was Ida.

Returning, once, from an afternoon's inspection of the great dry-dock building at Pearl Harbour, Lee Barton, driving his machine against time, in order to have time to dress for dinner, passed Sonny's car; and Sonny's one passenger, whom he was taking home, was Ida. One night, a week later, during which interval he had played no cards, he came home at eleven from a stag dinner at the University Club, just preceding Ida's return from the Alstone poi supper and dance. And Sonny had driven her home. Major Fanklin and his wife had first been dropped off by them, they mentioned, at Fort Shafter, on the other side of town and miles away from the beach.

Lee Barton, after all mere human man, as a human man unfailingly meeting Sonny in all friendliness, suffered poignantly in secret. Not even Ida dreamed that he suffered; and she went her merry, careless, laughing way, secure in her own heart, although a trifle perplexed at her husband's increase in number of pre-dinner cocktails.

Apparently, as always, she had access to almost all of him; but now she did not have access to his unguessable torment, nor to the long parallel columns of mental book-keeping running their totalling balances from moment to moment, day and night, in his brain. In one column were her undoubtable spontaneous expressions of her usual love and care for him, her many acts of comfort-serving and of advice-asking and advice-obeying. In another column, in which the items increasingly were entered, were her expressions and acts which he could not but classify as dubious. Were they what they seemed? Or were they of duplicity compounded, whether deliberately or unconsciously? The third column, longest of all, totalling most in human heart-appraisements, was filled with items relating directly or indirectly to her and Sonny Grandison. Lee Barton did not deliberately do this book-keeping. He could not help it. He would have liked to avoid it. But in his fairly ordered mind the items of entry, of themselves and quite beyond will on his part, took their places automatically in their respective columns.

In his distortion of vision, magnifying apparently trivial detail which half the time he felt he magnified, he had recourse to MacIlwaine, to whom he had once rendered a very considerable service. MacIlwaine was chief of detectives. "Is Sonny Grandison a womaning man?" Barton had demanded. MacIlwaine had said nothing. "Then he is a womaning man," had been Barton's declaration. And still the chief of detectives had said nothing.

Briefly afterward, ere he destroyed it as so much dynamite, Lee Barton went over the written report. Not bad, not really bad, was the summarization; but not too good after the death of his wife ten years before. That had been a love-match almost notorious in Honolulu society, because of the completeness of infatuation, not only before, but after marriage, and up to her tragic death when her horse fell with her a thousand feet off Nahiku Trail. And not for a long time afterward, MacIlwaine stated, had Grandison been guilty of interest in any woman. And whatever it was, it had been unvaryingly decent. Never a hint of gossip or scandal; and the entire community had come to accept that he was a one-woman man, and would never marry again. What small affairs MacIlwaine had jotted down he insisted that Sonny Grandison did not dream were known by another person outside the principals themselves.

Barton glanced hurriedly, almost shamedly, at the several names and incidents, and knew surprise ere he committed the document to the flames. At any rate, Sonny had been most discreet. As he stared at the ashes, Barton pondered how much of his own younger life, from his bachelor days, resided in old MacIlwaine's keeping. Next, Barton found himself blushing, to himself, at himself. If MacIlwaine knew so much of the private lives of community figures, then had not he, her husband and protector and shielder, planted in MacIlwaine's brain a suspicion of Ida?

"Anything on your mind?" Lee asked his wife that evening, as he stood holding her wrap while she put the last touches to her dressing.

This was in line with their old and successful compact of frankness, and he wondered, while he waited her answer, why he had refrained so long from asking her.

"No," she smiled. "Nothing particular. Afterwards . . . perhaps . . . "

She became absorbed in gazing at herself in the mirror, while she dabbed some powder on her nose and dabbed it off again.

"You know my way, Lee," she added, after the pause. "It takes me time to gather things together in my own way--when there are things to gather; but when I do, you always get them. And often there's nothing in them after all, I find, and so you are saved the nuisance of them."

She held out her arms for him to place the wrap about her--her valiant little arms that were so wise and steel-like in battling with the breakers, and that yet were such just mere-woman's arms, round and warm and white, delicious as a woman's arms should be, with the canny muscles, masking under soft-roundness of contour and fine smooth skin, capable of being flexed at will by the will of her.

He pondered her, with a grievous hurt and yearning of appreciation- -so delicate she seemed, so porcelain-fragile that a strong man could snap her in the crook of his arm.

"We must hurry!" she cried, as he lingered in the adjustment of the flimsy wrap over her flimsy-prettiness of gown. "We'll be late. And if it showers up Nuuanu, putting the curtains up will make us miss the second dance."

He made a note to observe with whom she danced that second dance, as she preceded him across the room to the door; while at the same time he pleasured his eye in what he had so often named to himself as the spirit-proud flesh-proud walk of her.

"You don't feel I'm neglecting you in my too-much poker?" he tried again, by indirection.

"Mercy, no! You know I just love you to have your card orgies. They're tonic for you. And you're so much nicer about them, so much more middle-aged. Why, it's almost years since you sat up later than one."

It did not shower up Nuuanu, and every overhead star was out in a clear trade-wind sky. In time at the Inchkeeps' for the second dance, Lee Barton observed that his wife danced it with Grandison-- which, of itself, was nothing unusual, but which became immediately a registered item in Barton's mental books.

An hour later, depressed and restless, declining to make one of a bridge foursome in the library and escaping from a few young matrons, he strolled out into the generous grounds. Across the lawn, at the far edge, he came upon the hedge of night-blooming cereus. To each flower, opening after dark and fading, wilting, perishing with the dawn, this was its one night of life. The great, cream-white blooms, a foot in diameter and more, lily-like and wax-like, white beacons of attraction in the dark, penetrating and seducing the night with their perfume, were busy and beautiful with their brief glory of living.

But the way along the hedge was populous with humans, two by two, male and female, stealing out between the dances or strolling the dances out, while they talked in low soft voices and gazed upon the wonder of flower-love. From the lanai drifted the love-caressing strains of "Hanalei" sung by the singing boys. Vaguely Lee Barton remembered--perhaps it was from some Maupassant story--the abbe, obsessed by the theory that behind all things were the purposes of God and perplexed so to interpret the night, who discovered at the last that the night was ordained for love.

The unanimity of the night as betrayed by flowers and humans was a hurt to Barton. He circled back toward the house along a winding path that skirted within the edge of shadow of the monkey-pods and algaroba trees. In the obscurity, where his path curved away into the open again, he looked across a space of a few feet where, on another path in the shadow, stood a pair in each other's arms. The impassioned low tones of the man had caught his ear and drawn his eyes, and at the moment of his glance, aware of his presence, the voice ceased, and the two remained immobile, furtive, in each other's arms.

He continued his walk, sombred by the thought that in the gloom of the trees was the next progression from the openness of the sky over those who strolled the night-flower hedge. Oh, he knew the game when of old no shadow was too deep, no ruse of concealment too furtive, to veil a love moment. After all, humans were like flowers, he meditated. Under the radiance from the lighted lanai, ere entering the irritating movement of life again to which he belonged, he paused to stare, scarcely seeing, at a flaunt of display of scarlet double-hibiscus blooms. And abruptly all that he was suffering, all that he had just observed, from the night- blooming hedge and the two-by-two love-murmuring humans to the pair like thieves in each other's arms, crystallized into a parable of life enunciated by the day-blooming hibiscus upon which he gazed, now at the end of its day. Bursting into its bloom after the dawn, snow-white, warming to pink under the hours of sun, and quickening to scarlet with the dark from which its beauty and its being would never emerge, it seemed to him that it epitomized man's life and passion.

What further connotations he might have drawn he was never to know; for from behind, in the direction of the algarobas and monkey-pods, came Ida's unmistakable serene and merry laugh. He did not look, being too afraid of what he knew he would see, but retreated hastily, almost stumbling, up the steps to the lanai. Despite that he knew what he was to see, when he did turn his head and beheld his wife and Sonny, the pair he had seen thieving in the dark, he went suddenly dizzy, and paused, supporting himself with a hand against a pillar, and smiling vacuously at the grouped singing boys who were pulsing the sensuous night into richer sensuousness with their honi kaua wiki-wiki refrain.

The next moment he had wet his lips with his tongue, controlled his face and flesh, and was bantering with Mrs. Inchkeep. But he could not waste time, or he would have to encounter the pair he could hear coming up the steps behind him.

"I feel as if I had just crossed the Great Thirst," he told his hostess, "and that nothing less than a high-ball will preserve me."

She smiled permission and nodded toward the smoking lanai, where they found him talking sugar politics with the oldsters when the dance began to break up.

Quite a party of half a dozen machines were starting for Waikiki, and he found himself billeted to drive the Leslies and Burnstons home, though he did not fail to note that Ida sat in the driver's seat with Sonny in Sonny's car. Thus, she was home ahead of him and brushing her hair when he arrived. The parting of bed-going was usual, on the face of it, although he was almost rigid in his successful effort for casualness as he remembered whose lips had pressed hers last before his.

Was, then, woman the utterly unmoral creature as depicted by the German pessimists? he asked himself, as he tossed under his reading lamp, unable to sleep or read. At the end of an hour he was out of bed, and into his medicine case. Five grains of opium he took straight. An hour later, afraid of his thoughts and the prospect of a sleepless night, he took another grain. At one-hour intervals he twice repeated the grain dosage. But so slow was the action of the drug that dawn had broken ere his eyes closed.

At seven he was awake again, dry-mouthed, feeling stupid and drowsy, yet incapable of dozing off for more than several minutes at a time. He abandoned the idea of sleep, ate breakfast in bed, and devoted himself to the morning papers and the magazines. But the drug effect held, and he continued briefly to doze through his eating and reading. It was the same when he showered and dressed, and, though the drug had brought him little forgetfulness during the night, he felt grateful for the dreaming lethargy with which it possessed him through the morning.

It was when his wife arose, her serene and usual self, and came in to him, smiling and roguish, delectable in her kimono, that the whim-madness of the opium in his system seized upon him. When she had clearly and simply shown that she had nothing to tell him under their ancient compact of frankness, he began building his opium lie. Asked how he had slept, he replied:

"Miserably. Twice I was routed wide awake with cramps in my feet. I was almost too afraid to sleep again. But they didn't come back, though my feet are sorer than blazes."

"Last year you had them," she reminded him.

"Maybe it's going to become a seasonal affliction," he smiled. "They're not serious, but they're horrible to wake up to. They won't come again till to-night, if they come at all, but in the meantime I feel as if I had been bastinadoed."

In the afternoon of the same day, Lee and Ida Barton made their shallow dive from the Outrigger beach, and went on, at a steady stroke, past the diving-stage to the big water beyond the Kanaka Surf. So quiet was the sea that when, after a couple of hours, they turned and lazily started shoreward through the Kanaka Surf they had it all to themselves. The breakers were not large enough to be exciting, and the last languid surf-boarders and canoeists had gone in to shore. Suddenly, Lee turned over on his back.

"What is it?" Ida called from twenty feet away.

"My foot--cramp," he answered calmly, though the words were twisted out through clenched jaws of control.

The opium still had its dreamy way with him, and he was without excitement. He watched her swimming toward him with so steady and unperturbed a stroke that he admired her own self-control, although at the same time doubt stabbed him with the thought that it was because she cared so little for him, or, rather, so much immediately more for Grandison.

"Which foot?" she asked, as she dropped her legs down and began treading water beside him.

"The left one--ouch! Now it's both of them."

He doubled his knees, as if involuntarily raised his head and chest forward out of the water, and sank out of sight in the down-wash of a scarcely cresting breaker. Under no more than a brief several seconds, he emerged spluttering and stretched out on his back again.

Almost he grinned, although he managed to turn the grin into a pain-grimace, for his simulated cramp had become real. At least in one foot it had, and the muscles convulsed painfully.

"The right is the worst," he muttered, as she evinced her intention of laying hands on his cramp and rubbing it out. "But you'd better keep away. I've had cramps before, and I know I'm liable to grab you if these get any worse."

Instead, she laid her hands on the hard-knotted muscles, and began to rub and press and bend.

"Please," he gritted through his teeth. "You must keep away. Just let me lie out here--I'll bend the ankle and toe-joints in the opposite ways and make it pass. I've done it before and know how to work it."

She released him, remaining close beside him and easily treading water, her eyes upon his face to judge the progress of his own attempt at remedy. But Lee Barton deliberately bent joints and tensed muscles in the directions that would increase the cramp. In his bout the preceding year with the affliction, he had learned, lying in bed and reading when seized, to relax and bend the cramps away without even disturbing his reading. But now he did the thing in reverse, intensifying the cramp, and, to his startled delight, causing it to leap into his right calf. He cried out with anguish, apparently lost control of himself, attempted to sit up, and was washed under by the next wave.

He came up, spluttered, spread-eagled on the surface, and had his knotted calf gripped by the strong fingers of both Ida's small hands.

"It's all right," she said, while she worked. "No cramp like this lasts very long."

"I didn't know it could be so savage," he groaned. "If only it doesn't go higher! It makes one feel so helpless."

He gripped the biceps of both her arms in a sudden spasm, attempting to climb out upon her as a drowning man might try to climb out on an oar and sinking her down under him. In the struggle under water, before he permitted her to wrench clear, her rubber cap was torn off, and her hairpins pulled out, so that she came up gasping for air and half-blinded by her wet-clinging hair. Also, he was certain he had surprised her into taking in a quantity of water.

"Keep away!" he warned, as he spread-eagled with acted desperateness.

But her fingers were deep into the honest pain-wrack of his calf, and in her he could observe no reluctance of fear.

"It's creeping up," he grunted through tight teeth, the grunt itself a half-controlled groan.

He stiffened his whole right leg, as with another spasm, hurting his real minor cramps, but flexing the muscles of his upper leg into the seeming hardness of cramp.

The opium still worked in his brain, so that he could play-act cruelly, while at the same time he appraised and appreciated her stress of control and will that showed in her drawn face, and the terror of death in her eyes, with beyond it and behind it, in her eyes and through her eyes, the something more of the spirit of courage, and higher thought, and resolution.

Still further, she did not enunciate so cheap a surrender as, "I'll die with you." Instead, provoking his admiration, she did say, quietly: "Relax. Sink until only your lips are out. I'll support your head. There must be a limit to cramp. No man ever died of cramp on land. Then in the water no strong swimmer should die of cramp. It's bound to reach its worst and pass. We're both strong swimmers and cool-headed--"

He distorted his face and deliberately dragged her under. But when they emerged, still beside him, supporting his head as she continued to tread water, she was saying:

"Relax. Take it easy. I'll hold your head up. Endure it. Live through it. Don't fight it. Make yourself slack--slack in your mind; and your body will slack. Yield. Remember how you taught me to yield to the undertow."

An unusually large breaker for so mild a surf curled overhead, and he climbed out on her again, sinking both of them under as the wave-crest over-fell and smashed down.

"Forgive me," he mumbled through pain clenched teeth, as they drew in their first air again. "And leave me." He spoke jerkily, with pain-filled pauses between his sentences. "There is no need for both of us to drown. I've got to go. It will be in my stomach, at any moment, and then I'll drag you under, and be unable to let go of you. Please, please, dear, keep away. One of us is enough. You've plenty to live for."

She looked at him in reproach so deep that the last vestige of the terror of death was gone from her eyes. It was as if she had said, and more than if she had said: "I have only you to live for."

Then Sonny did not count with her as much as he did!--was Barton's exultant conclusion. But he remembered her in Sonny's arms under the monkey-pods and determined on further cruelty. Besides, it was the lingering opium in him that suggested this cruelty. Since he had undertaken this acid test, urged the poppy juice, then let it be a real acid test.

He doubled up and went down, emerged, and apparently strove frantically to stretch out in the floating position. And she did not keep away from him.

"It's too much!" he groaned, almost screamed. "I'm losing my grip. I've got to go. You can't save me. Keep away and save yourself."

But she was to him, striving to float his mouth clear of the salt, saying: "It's all right. It's all right. The worst is right now. Just endure it a minute more, and it will begin to ease."

He screamed out, doubled, seized her, and took her down with him. And he nearly did drown her, so well did he play-act his own drowning. But never did she lose her head nor succumb to the fear of death so dreadfully imminent. Always, when she got her head out, she strove to support him while she panted and gasped encouragement in terms of: "Relax . . . Relax . . . Slack . . . Slack out . . . At any time . . . now . . . you'll pass . . . the worst . . . No matter how much it hurts . . . it will pass . . . You're easier now . . . aren't you?"

And then he would put her down again, going from bad to worse--in his ill-treatment of her; making her swallow pints of salt water, secure in the knowledge that it would not definitely hurt her. Sometimes they came up for brief emergences, for gasping seconds in the sunshine on the surface, and then were under again, dragged under by him, rolled and tumbled under by the curling breakers.

Although she struggled and tore herself from his grips, in the times he permitted her freedom she did not attempt to swim away from him, but, with fading strength and reeling consciousness, invariably came to him to try to save him. When it was enough, in his judgment, and more than enough, he grew quieter, left her released, and stretched out on the surface.

"A-a-h," he sighed long, almost luxuriously, and spoke with pauses for breath. "It is passing. It seems like heaven. My dear, I'm water-logged, yet the mere absence of that frightful agony makes my present state sheerest bliss."

She tried to gasp a reply, but could not.

"I'm all right," he assured her. "Let us float and rest up. Stretch out, yourself, and get your wind back."

And for half an hour, side by side, on their backs, they floated in the fairly placid Kanaka Surf. Ida Barton was the first to announce recovery by speaking first.

"And how do you feel now, man of mine?" she asked.

"I feel as if I'd been run over by a steam-roller," he replied. "And you, poor darling?"

"I feel I'm the happiest woman in the world. I'm so happy I could almost cry, but I'm too happy even for that. You had me horribly frightened for a time. I thought I was to lose you."

Lee Barton's heart pounded up. Never a mention of losing herself. This, then, was love, and all real love, proved true--the great love that forgot self in the loved one.

"And I'm the proudest man in the world," he told her; "because my wife is the bravest woman in the world."

"Brave!" she repudiated. "I love you. I never knew how much, how really much, I loved you as when I was losing you. And now let's work for shore. I want you all alone with me, your arms around me, while I tell you all you are to me and shall always be to me."

In another half-hour, swimming strong and steadily, they landed on the beach and walked up the hard wet sand among the sand-loafers and sun-baskers.

"What were the two of you doing out there?" queried one of the Outrigger captains. "Cutting up?"

"Cutting up," Ida Barton answered with a smile.

"We're the village cut-ups, you know," was Lee Barton's assurance.

That evening, the evening's engagement cancelled, found the two, in a big chair, in each other's arms.

"Sonny sails to-morrow noon," she announced casually and irrelevant to anything in the conversation. "He's going out to the Malay Coast to inspect what's been done with that lumber and rubber company of his."

"First I've heard of his leaving us," Lee managed to say, despite his surprise.

"I was the first to hear of it," she added. "He told me only last night."

"At the dance?"

She nodded.

"Rather sudden, wasn't it?"

"Very sudden." Ida withdrew herself from her husband's arms and sat up. "And I want to talk to you about Sonny. I've never had a real secret from you before. I didn't intend ever to tell you. But it came to me to-day, out in the Kanaka Surf, that if we passed out, it would be something left behind us unsaid."

She paused, and Lee, half-anticipating what was coming, did nothing to help her, save to girdle and press her hand in his.

"Sonny rather lost his . . . his head over me," she faltered. "Of course, you must have noticed it. And . . . and last night, he wanted me to run away with him. Which isn't my confession at all . . . "

Still Lee Barton waited.

"My confession," she resumed, "is that I wasn't the least bit angry with him--only sorrowful and regretful. My confession is that I rather slightly, only rather more than slightly, lost my own head. That was why I was kind and gentle to him last night. I am no fool. I knew it was due. And--oh, I know, I'm just a feeble female of vanity compounded--I was proud to have such a man swept off his feet by me, by little me. I encouraged him. I have no excuse. Last night would not have happened had I not encouraged him. And I, and not he, was the sinner last night when he asked me. And I told him no, impossible, as you should know why without my repeating it to you. And I was maternal to him, very much maternal. I let him take me in his arms, let myself rest against him, and, for the first time because it was to be the for-ever last time, let him kiss me and let myself kiss him. You . . . I know you understand . . . it was his renunciation. And I didn't love Sonny. I don't love him. I have loved you, and you only, all the time."

She waited, and felt her husband's arm pass around her shoulder and under her own arm, and yielded to his drawing down of her to him.

"You did have me worried more than a bit," he admitted, "until I was afraid I was going to lose you. And . . . " He broke off in patent embarrassment, then gripped the idea courageously. "Oh, well, you know you're my one woman. Enough said."

She fumbled the match-box from his pocket and struck a match to enable him to light his long-extinct cigar.

"Well," he said, as the smoke curled about them, "knowing you as I know you, and ALL of you, all I can say is that I'm sorry for Sonny for what he's missed--awfully sorry for him, but equally glad for me. And . . . one other thing: five years hence I've something to tell you, something rich, something ridiculously rich, and all about me and the foolishness of me over you. Five years. Is it a date?"

"I shall keep it if it is fifty years," she sighed, as she nestled closer to him.

GLEN ELLEN, CALIFORNIA. August 17, 1916.

THE END

www.ingramcontent.com/pod-product-compliance
Lightning Source LLC
LaVergne TN
LVHW071117170125
801546LV00024B/489